I0532716

Grave Markers
Volume 2

Hal Bodner, Sebastian Bendix,

and Russell Coy

A
Grinning Skull Press
Publication

Compilation Copyright © 2016 Grinning Skull Press

All rights reserved. No part of this book may be used or reproduced in any manner whatsoever without written permission except in the case of brief quotations embodied in critical articles or reviews.

This book contains works of fiction. All characters depicted in this book are fictitious, and any resemblance to real persons—living or dead—is purely coincidental.

"Tolerance" copyright ©2016 Hal Bodner
    Originally published by Grinning Skull Press, February 29, 2016
"Shriek of the Harpy" copyright ©2016 Sebastian Bendix
    Originally published by Grinning Skull Press, May 17, 2016
"The One Who Lies Next to You" copyright ©2016 Russell Coy
    Originally published by Grinning Skull Press, November 26, 2016

The Skull logo with stylized lettering was created for Grinning Skull Press by Dan Moran, http://dan-moran-art.com/.
Cover designed by Jeffrey Kosh, http://jeffreykosh.wix.com/jeffreykoshgraphics.

ISBN: 0-9984055-6-6
ISBN-13: 978-0-9984055-6-8

CONTENTS

A WORD ABOUT GRAVE MARKERS

I promise to keep this short so you can get on to reading the tales collected in this volume. Folks often ask about Grave Markers and what they are. Grave Markers are, in a word, novelettes. They are stories too long to be included in anthologies (which usually average 5,000 to 7,000 words) but not quite long enough to be published on their own as stand-alone novellas. They are published individually in digital formats, and then later compiled into a print collection. The reason why we started this line is we often heard authors commenting that there wasn't a market for those "in-between" length stories and we wanted to give them an outlet for such pieces. And that about sums it up. Told you I'd keep it short. Now, without further ado, I present to you the premier collection of Grave Markers. Enjoy!

Michael J. Evans
Grinning Skull Press

GRAVE MARKER

A WEST HOLLYWOOD VAMPIRE
NOVELETTE

HAL BODNER

TOLERANCE

WELCOME TO WEST HOLLYWOOD

In the mid-80s, Zelda Rubinstein was featured in a series of ads for AIDS awareness. In each ad, she was dressed as a stereotypical apron-clad housewife who was advising her son to play safely. What made the ads so memorable that I can remember them 30 years later when I can't even remember what I had for breakfast this morning? It was Zelda, a diminutive actress with a BIG personality. They were quirky, which is kind of how I imagined the actress would be in real life.

You might find yourself wondering how this ties in with Hal Bodner's *West Hollywood Vampire* series. Well, after talking with the author about what West Hollywood was like, it was one of the first things to come to mind. Why? Because it was quirky. I mean, how else would you describe a city that at one time had a gay porn star as its mayor. A city that houses not just one, but eight (or is it nine?) doggy hotels. A city that has just as many billboards advertising personal lubricant and safe condom use as it does for shampoos and fast food restaurants. A city that houses a single movie theater — the Tom Katt (named after a gay porn star), which only shows...? You guessed it!

Quirky.

Which brings me to the cast of characters who make up Mr. Bodner's series: Pamela Berman, Becky O'Brien, and Troy Raleigh to name a few.

I first had the pleasure of meeting these characters about ten years ago when I picked up a copy of *Bite Club*. I have to admit I wasn't expecting much when I started it. It was the author's first novel, which wasn't the cause for the low expectations; it was the fact that the book

3

was slapped with a "gay" label, and most gay-oriented fiction I'd read to that point had been boring and badly written, but it was vampires, so I *had* to read it. And oh, what a treat!

For those unfamiliar with the book, it deals with a series of gruesome murders. Somebody is killing off West Hollywood's handsome young men, and it's up to Coroner Becky O'Brien to figure out how. She admits to being stumped because all the evidence suggests something that couldn't possibly exist: vampires! As a last recourse, she calls an old friend, Christopher Driscoll, who is an expert on serial killers, and asks for his help, not realizing that her "old" friend is a lot older than she thinks he is. When Chris arrives in West Hollywood with his Renfield/lover, Troy, in tow, the trio find themselves pitted against a supernatural serial killer, and the only chance they have of defeating this monster is for Chris to reveal his true nature.

Sounds like a straight up horror/mystery, and it would be without the help of Troy and Pamela. Where Troy is concerned, forget everything you know (or think you know) about Renfields (and please don't use that word around him). Troy Raleigh is sexy (and he knows it), somewhat flamboyant (maybe that's an understatement), and has a mouth that doesn't know when to stop. Add to the mix Pamela Berman, the irascible City Councilwoman with an affinity for garish clothing and who has a cause for every minute of the day, and you have a recipe for disaster in less-talented hands, but Bodner's craftsmanship blends the horror and the comedic seamlessly. By the time I finished the book, I was instantly a fan and I waited eagerly for the next book to come out.

And I waited.

And waited.

And waited.

In the meantime, along came Facebook and I decided to see if Mr. Bodner had a presence there. Sure enough, there he was. Without hesitation, I sent him a friend request. What follows (thanks to Facebook's extensive memory, which isn't as blond as Hal's) is our first contact back in April of 2009:

HB: Okay... So, tell me... Who ARE you? Do we know each other? WHC? HWA? Necon? I'm blond. The memory is blonder.
ME: We've never met. Just a fan if you are the Hal Bodner who

wrote Bite Club. I'm an aspiring writer with a number of projects I'm currently working on and just trying to network with other writers.

HB: A FAN?????!!!!!????? We LIKE fans! We even sleep with them on occasion if they're cute! (Not really, but it makes a nice promo line, doesn't it? <G>)

So.... tell me, tell me. How'd ya like Bite Club? Stroke me, baby, stroke me. (I have a TREMENDOUS....er...um... ego. Yeah! That's it. It's a big EGO and NOT what you were thinking I was gonna say!)

(And ever the salesman, he had to make the pitch for his latest book)

> **HB:** Seriously, have you read *In Flesh & Stone* yet? Yes, it's soft-core porn -- well, NOT so "soft". But it's also a pretty damned fine novel ...

(portion of irrelevant dialogue deleted, then he went on to answer the question I had yet to ask: Would there ever be another Chris and Troy novel?)

> **HB:** There are two more Chris & Troy books done and a fourth in the works, *Wild About Hairy*, *Mummy Dearest*, and *I've Got You Into Your Skin*.

(more irrelevant dialogue deleted)

> **HB:** So, how'd ya like the book? Inquiring minds wanna know and all that!

I knew right away I was going to like this guy. (I also curse the day I met him because he's the reason my TBR pile has grown exponentially. Yeah, I bought a Kindle because, at the time, *In Flesh & Stone* was only available in digital formats.)

Knowing there were more Chris and Troy books coming, all I had to do was wait.

And wait.

And wait.

And finally, in 2012, *The Trouble with Hairy*, the second Chris and Troy novel, came out! I was giddy with anticipation, one, because it was finally here, and two, because this one was about werewolves (my favorite of the iconic monsters), so if you like 'em talk, dark, and furry, head on over to Amazon and grab yourself a copy. Sadly, however, *Hairy* didn't come close to being as good as *Bite Club*; in fact, it surpassed it! All of our favorite characters are back, and we are introduced to some new ones: Carlos, assistant to Berman and who also happens to worship the ground the cantankerous Councilwoman walks on, and Shanda Leer, his drag queen alter ego, who shapes her appearance on Berman herself; Louis, the werewolf; and Scotty, the ghoul. We're also allowed to get closer to some of our favorite characters; we see that there's more to Berman than just a disgruntled old woman, we get a bit of Troy's history, and we feel for Becky as she looks for love in all the wrong places.

And then the waiting game began anew as the world waited for the release of *Mummy, Dearest*, which, by the way, Hal assures me is in the works.

In 2013, I had the pleasure of meeting Mr. Bodner in person at NECON, and among the things we talked about was West Hollywood Vampires. I was surprised to learn that Becky, not Chris, was originally supposed to be the central character of *Bite Club*. While she's a great character, I couldn't see her carrying the series and was glad that the focus shifted away from Becky and onto Chris and Troy. We also talked about the future of the series, as it seemed that gay-oriented horror/comedy was a hard sell in the publishing world. Hal had ventured into the waters of self-publishing with *The Trouble with Hairy*, and as popular as *Bite Club* was, being one of the highest earners for its publisher at the time, *Hairy* didn't have the success that *Bite Club* had had. So it seemed that the future of the series was now in limbo. But to show me he hadn't given up the characters of Chris and Troy altogether, Hal had sent me the story you are about to read. In it we are introduced to yet another new character, **Razmussen**, a new arrival in West Hollywood, and like most immigrants, Raz was eager to set up shop so as not to be a burden on his new homeland. But given Razmussen's nature, the local new eatery might not have been such a good idea, especially when the children start disappearing.

Finding it a home, however, was proving to be problematic, not because of the subject matter, which some might find particularly gruesome, but because of the length. Coming in at approximately 10k words, it was too long for most anthologies, but not long enough to be published as a stand-alone novella, so it languished in a drawer.

Recently, we here at Grinning Skull Press wanted to experiment with a new line that we call Grave Markers. The line is intended for pieces such as "Tolerance," too long for one market but not long enough for the other. They would be released individually in digital format, and early the following year, all the Grave Markers published the previous year would be compiled into a print collection. When Hal heard about this, he asked if we would be willing to include "Tolerance" in the line, and we were honored. So without further ado, I give you Hal Bodner's "Tolerance, a West Hollywood Vampires novelette". I hope you enjoy it as much as we did.

—Michael J. Evans
Grinning Skull Press

CHAPTER ONE

"Please tell me you're not bringing him more bad news. You know how compulsive Captain Anderson gets when he's upset. I had to stop him from trying to iron some crumpled arrest reports."

Coroner Becky O'Brien did not like the way the secretary looked at all. Haggard was a good description, notwithstanding the hopefulness of Claire's expression. Stress was already in the process of turning her crow's feet into something more substantial; raven's feet seemed like a good probability, or perhaps the talons of a small eagle.

"I heard. That's why I came over. I was thinking about hijacking him and heading over to that new restaurant on the corner of West Knoll and Santa Monica. You been there yet?"

Claire shook her head, mournfully. "These kidnappings have us all so crazy. Everyone in the department has been living on take-out." She risked a glance down the hall of the Sheriff's Station as if expecting to see someone lurking there. Satisfied that the corridor was empty, she lowered her voice to a stage whisper. "One of the deputies managed to sneak a microwave into the men's locker room. After we got sick of pizza and Chinese, we could heat casseroles from home."

"No!" Becky had difficulty wrapping her mind around the concept of anyone possibly tiring of Chinese take-out, especially when Kung Pao Bistro made the most delicious Honey Walnut Shrimp with just a hint of...

"I don't know how *she* found out." Clair interrupted the coroner's calorie-packed reverie. "But when she did, there was hell to pay."

Becky smiled sympathetically, knowing that the *she* in question was Pamela Burman, West Hollywood's irascible and irritable City Manager. Less than a year ago, Burman and her nemesis, Mayor Daniel Eversleigh, had finally agreed on something. In public, she claimed she loathed the mayor because of his legendary incompetence. Privately, she blamed her enmity on pheromones. In particular, she told anyone who would listen that Eversleigh exuded some invisible miasma, far below the level of the human sense of smell, which compelled her to want to scratch her fists on his face. The battles between them were epic and, whenever a council meeting was televised, the local cable channel could bank on increased ratings. Throughout the city, residents would tune in with ghoulish glee, eager to witness each new feat of pugilistic abandon when the two elected officials faced off.

By purest ironic coincidence, the kind of ironic coincidence that causes icebergs to cripple reputedly unsinkable ocean liners, both Burman and Eversleigh despised microwaves, albeit for different reasons.

Daniel inevitably pandered to whatever constituency he felt would best serve to reelect him. Unfortunately, the majority vote in West Hollywood was inevitably aligned with political positions best described as

Far Out in Left Field. Fresh from their success in banning non-bio-degradable styrofoam from within the city limits, and still trumpeting their glee at having upped the penalties for illegal tree trimming to include jail time, the concerned citizens had turned their sights to banishing evil microwaves from city-operated facilities.

Pamela Burman agreed with the result, if not the motivation. She was convinced that invisible emanations from modern devices caused brain cancer. Had she her druthers, she would have personally destroyed every citizen's cell phone and erected lead barriers rivaling the Great Wall of China around the city, thereby blocking all WiFi and satellite television signals. Recognizing that even WeHo's progressive population might revolt if she got her way, she contented herself with reluctantly joining forces with Daniel to eliminate the brain-destroying waves from municipal kitchens.

The local supermarkets were delighted with the increased lunch hour rush from city employees who were used to popping a cup of organic non-GMO ramen or a certified SUSTAINABLE entree into the microwave. Most city workers were happy to pay slightly more for their lunches, knowing that their supermarket sandwich featured the breast of a chicken, hand fed on tofu, that had been humanely allowed to die of old age.

"It was lovely while we had it," Claire said, her eyes shining with the kind of wistful melancholia that originates only from the memory of a confiscated kitchen appliance. "We considered setting up a hibachi in the parking lot. A few of the boys in Vice were gonna re-purpose the obsolete paper files from the archives as fuel. But we were worried she'd slap us with a citation for air pollution." She shrugged regret-fully. "The duty sergeant wanted to use the leftover dummies from the last time she tried burning the mayor in effigy, but no one wanted to encourage her to make more."

Claire gestured toward the Captain's office door.

"Go on in. And if you can think of any way to cheer him up...?"

CHAPTER TWO

If Claire looked tired, the puffy pockets under Captain Clive Anderson's eyes were larger than swag bags at the Oscars.

"You," Becky announced even before she'd finished settling her bulk into a chair, "have been working way too hard. That's my professional medical opinion, by the way."

She opened her ubiquitous black bag and started rummaging through it. Within a shockingly short span of time, the top of Anderson's desk displayed an impressive array of crumpled notepaper, several pairs of latex gloves, a can of dietetic chocolate shake, a half-eaten Snicker's bar, three syringes, a torn zip lock bag leaking trail mix made with M&Ms, a key ring large enough to unlock every door of Godzilla's house, a half-dozen mangled protein bars, a parking citation, and a large iced cupcake that had been ineffectively wrapped in plastic film and which still oozed impressive blobs of bright pink icing.

"I keep meaning to pay that." She guiltily snatched up the ticket and jammed it back into her bag. "This is what I was looking for. Drink up."

She thrust a small violent purple and garish yellow bottle across the desk.

Clive sighed at the mélange of detritus, crumbs, and medical supplies.

"Why is it that within five minutes of you traipsing into my office, it looks like the space station crashed into my desk?" He gingerly picked up a desiccated felt tip pen and tentatively poked it at the cupcake.

"Aren't you supposed to be dieting again?"

"Oh! Yeah! Right!" Her hand vanished into her bag and reappeared with a wormy green apple, followed by something that might recently have been a banana.

"Fruit! It's healthy. I knew I had some in here somewhere. As of three weeks ago, I've lost almost forty-five pounds," she boasted.

"Oh really?" Using only the tips of two manicured fingernails, he picked up the Snickers bar and examined it critically. "On the caramel and fudge diet?" Grimacing with distaste, he held the treat above his waste basket and paused to make his point before dropping it into the can.

"Hey! That was still good!" came the protest, followed by a sheepish, "Never mind. I have a bunch more in the freezer back at the morgue. So, aren't you gonna drink that?"

Clive eyed the garish bottle doubtfully. "What is it? Liquid Easter eggs?"

"It's an energy drink. Low-cal. I bought a bunch for some reason that now eludes me. I can't stand 'em." She paused in the middle of peeling the banana when she saw Clive looking askance at the almost-midnight blackness of the fruit. "If you let 'em get super ripe, it allows all the sugars to develop," she announced with some defiance.

"Becky." Clive held out the wastebasket and waited.

"Drink your energy drink. You look like shit."

"The..." He grimaced and shook the trashcan. "The banana first. That *is* a banana, right?"

"It was." Becky seemed doubtful. The peel had all but fallen off and a sort of brownish goo, smelling pungently of vastly overripe banana, now covered her fingers. "I suppose it's a little past its sell-by date."

With not a little reluctance, she threw the fruit away. Her eyes flitted to the desk and her expression brightened when she saw the cupcake. Before she could get her hands on it, Clive snatched it up, along with the broken bag of trail mix and the battered protein bars and threw them out as well. Without another word, he strode to his office door, basket in hand.

"Claire? Would you mind dealing with this before it starts to stink? Apparently, our beloved coroner is on a fruit diet this time. One more thing..."

He marched back to his desk and grabbed the little purple bottle and turned it over to Claire as well. "Be careful of this one. Even Becky doesn't like the taste so..." He closed his eyes with a momentary shudder. "I can only imagine."

"Really?" Claire seemed surprised. She moved her reading glasses from the top of her head to the bridge of her nose and peered at the label. "The first ingredient is high fructose corn syrup. Are you sure?" She directed the question at Becky.

"She's sure," Clive answered for her. He closed the door and resumed his seat again.

"Aren't we all Mister I'm-In-Control since overcoming our little werewolf phobia?"

"I'm not in the mood, Becky. Nothing personal."

"Tell Mama all about it," she quipped, settling herself more comfortably and ignoring the way the chair's legs creaked. While she had indeed lost a substantial amount of weight, she was still far from svelte. Though her girth alone was insufficient to do much damage, her habit of enthusiastically hurling herself into the chair like a ton and a half of Tastykakes wreaked havoc on the furniture. Every time she visited, Clive winced in anticipation of the legs collapsing and spilling her onto the floor.

"I'm guessing you're getting a shit-ton of pressure to solve these kidnappings."

"You have no idea." He busied himself separating the unused medical supplies from the opened packages, smoothing out the crumpled notes and sorting through the other junk. "I'm getting it from all sides. The mayor, Pamela, the Chamber of Commerce, and every damned Neighborhood Watch in the city."

Idly, he uncapped a pen and tested it by scrawling a non-existent doodle on a scrap of paper. Finding the ink dry, he made as if to toss it away before he realized he'd given Clair his waste can. He placed it neatly on the far side of his desk, uncapped another, and repeated the process.

"Don't you ever throw *anything* out?"

"I forget." She shrugged. "If you're finished being all judgmental about what I keep in my purse..."

"That's a purse? I thought it was a black hole with diarrhea."

"If you're *quite* finished," she scowled. "Talk to me about the kids.

Clive abandoned his fussing. He steepled his fingers in front of his face and rested his chin in the crook between his thumbs and his index fingers.

"Seven have gone missing in the past week. People are frantic."

"*Seven?* Wow! I mean, I heard about...let me see..." She rapidly ticked off numbers on her fingers. "About three of them. But... seven? I'll *bet* people are frantic. How come Ed Larsen at the *Gay Gazette* hasn't gone crazy?"

Clive spared her a withering glare, making it clear that he believed her IQ had suddenly dropped fifty points.

"This is West Hollywood, Becky. Larsen's been preoccupied with running those editorials about that new Mexican cantina."

"The one with the neon sign that encourages animal cruelty because it shows a fish jumping into a margarita glass?"

"Yeah. The outcry has been huge. Apparently, next to a goldfish drowning in tequila, a couple of missing kids is no big deal." He didn't bother to hide his disgust with Larsen's peculiar notion of what qualified as news. "In the meantime, I've hauled in every registered sex offender in the city."

Becky looked puzzled.

"The pedophile angle," he explained. "And let me tell you, there's been an outcry about *that*, too. More than three-quarters of the people we interviewed have twenty-year-old criminal records for nothing worse than propositioning an undercover cop or holding hands in a gay bar. You'd have to be crazy to prosecute those cases anymore. Don't get me wrong. We came across some real creeps as well. Two of them, in particular, made my Spider Sense tingle and we'll keep an eye on them. But the rest all checked out clean. No parole violations. Nada. We're shooting blanks."

"You started a curfew?"

"Three days ago. We're still losing a kid a day. Poof! Vanished! Well, not quite. We got through last Tuesday without a problem. But there were two kids on Monday to make up for it. Twins."

"Clive..." She leaned over his desk and accidentally rested her elbow in a smudge of pink icing that he'd missed when he tossed out the cupcake. "I don't mean to minimize the tragedy, but you look like hell. When was the last time you ate?"

"I had a sandwich... this morning," he responded vaguely.

"That settles it. I'm taking you to lunch at Yo-Ogert-T."

"At... what?" Clive looked at her like she was crazy. "Wait. Don't tell me. You mistook embalming fluid for orange soda again."

"Cute. Very cute. I'm an M.E. Not a funeral director. No one gets embalmed at the morgue." She positioned her bag just below the edge of the desk so that she could easily sweep the objects that Clive had painstakingly sorted through back into her purse in a disorganized mess once again.

"The yogurt shop over on West Knoll. They're serving lunch now. My assistant, Ty, tells me they have the best barbecue this side of East LA. He should know, he's from Texas."

"He's Japanese, Becky. He knows sushi."

"By way of Texas," Becky corrected firmly.

"Wait," Clive frowned when something rang a mental bell. "West Knoll? That new super trendy place? The one that's been overrun with movie stars and hipsters?"

"It might be." She shifted in her chair and avoided making eye contact.

"Becky, the idiots on the Business License Commission approved this joint in a residential zone. Without parking! The neighbors have been complaining about customers parking wherever the hell they can. My deputies started an illegal betting pool to see who can ticket the most Oscar winners for blocking the street. Tinkerbell Towing is practically about to do a public stock offering because their revenues have gone up from hauling so many limos and Jaguars off of people's front lawns! Last week, a customer forgot to set the handbrake on his Hummer and when he came out with his yogurt, the damned thing had rolled into someone's swimming pool. Do you have any idea of what kind of scandal we'd have if anyone saw my car there? Or worse, your van? There's already a petition going around to revoke your driver's license. Between the owner of that pizza parlor you smashed into and the way you and your little friends destroyed all that munici-pal art last time..."

"All *right!*" If it was possible to shout through gritted teeth, Becky was doing it. She took a deep breath and forced an insincere smile. "We'll walk."

CHAPTER THREE

"It's still a stupid name," Clive grumbled as soon as he'd swallowed another mouthful of meat slathered with spicy sauce. "But I gotta hand it to them. I've had some good barbecue in my time and this may be the best I ever tasted."

"You do realize that people are looking at you, right?"

His eyebrows rose, silently questioning as he sliced off a small portion of bun, dipped it in sauce, and placed it onto his tongue. He sighed with culinary pleasure.

"It's sacrilegious, eating it like that. You're supposed to use your hands." She held up her fingers, which were liberally drenched with sauce, and waggled them. Clive winced as droplets of liquefied tomato spattered across the table. "Doing it *your* way," she shuddered, "is like using a knife and fork to eat pizza."

"Some of us like the food to go *in* our mouths, Becky."

He used his knife to gesture at the accumulated stains that had appeared on the coroner's blouse within seconds of her first bite. From long experience, Clive had arranged a veritable curtain of paper napkins as a bib to cover his own front, hoping to shield himself from the onslaught of dining with Becky O'Brien. It wouldn't protect him completely, but he figured his dry cleaner hadn't had a good challenge in quite a while — since the last time he'd dined with the coroner, in fact.

"One of these days," he suggested, not unkindly, "you may wanna haul yourself over to the Pacific Design Center and see if you can convince one of those bright young fashion folks to whip you up something in a nice oil cloth."

A jet of tomato sauce and chopped onion shot from the opposite end of Becky's sandwich when she chomped down on it. Half landed on the table and half made an unerring beeline for the sole remaining unstained spot on her blouse.

"Or maybe Teflon."

"Eat it like a dweeb, if that's what you want. Oh my gosh! This Louisiana Sweet and Hot sauce is the *best*! You're gonna have to cuff me to keep me from ordering another."

"What about dessert? That fabulous yogurt you were raving about on the way over? I know it's asking a lot, but do you think you could manage to save some room."

"There is that," she replied. Her eyes swept to the menu board posted above the counter and her expression vacillated between wistful regret while she once again perused the sandwich choices and anticipatory bliss when she greedily eyed the yogurt flavors.

Just before Clive returned to his meticulous evisceration of his sandwich, he happened to glance over Becky's shoulder. When he saw who had just walked into the shop, his normally dark brown skin paled to the color of chocolate that has been sitting too long in the fridge and developed a bloom of milk fat.

"I suspect," he all but moaned, "that we're about to be joined by a couple of your friends."

Becky shifted so that she had a better angle from which to see the door and waved wildly. "Over here! Hey! Over here!"

"Must you do that?" the Captain hissed. "Don't I have enough trouble right now? You know what happens whenever those two get going?"

"Those two have saved our asses a couple of times," Becky reminded him. "It could be worse. At least Louis isn't with them."

"I actually *like* Louis," Clive said plaintively. "Once you get past him using your good loafers as chew toys, he's a very likable young man."

"Fancy meeting you here."

Christopher Driscoll almost always smiled more with his eyes than with his mouth, for obvious reasons. He greeted them with one of his odd little bows. "Mind if we join you?"

Resigned, Clive slid aside to make room.

"Becky and frozen yogurt." The bright and chirpy comment from the short, tight-bodied blond who accompanied the vampire was layered with sweet bitchiness. "Like that's a stretch."

"Behave, Troy," Chris reprimanded almost absently as he sat down. "Or you can't have extra toppings."

The Southern boy affected a stubborn moue of haughty pique.

22

On anyone else the expression would have been unattractive, but even while doing his best to channel the Wicked Witch of the West, Troy Raleigh was incapable of looking anything other than adorable.

"I'll get you something, too. What flavor?"

Chris arched one eyebrow and said sardonically, "Like it matters?"

"That means two double scoops for me!" Troy crowed. Since the vampire was already seated, Troy had to bend slightly to kiss him on the mouth. "I knew there were advantages to marrying you. Ta ta!"

"No more hundred dollar tips!" Chris called after him. He caught Clive's and Becky's questioning looks and explained, "He thinks the Russian boy behind the counter is cute. The one with all the biceps. He tipped him twice and told him he could...er... deliver anytime. Last Tuesday night, he showed up at our place dressed like a porn star to drop off Troy's order. While I would have appreciated it at almost any other time, I was already in the middle of dinner and the interruption was..." He grinned and flashed a hint of fang, which caused Clive to pale even more. "Awkward."

"Dressed as a porn star?" Becky scrunched up her face. "But porn stars don't..."

"Exactly."

"Oh!" Then something else her friend had said registered. "De-livery!" Blissful happiness suffused her face at the notion of the frozen confection being on-call twenty-four hours a day.

"If you like," Chris said, "I can talk to Razmussen and ask him if he can schedule a weekly drop off at the morgue. It's not like you don't have enough freezer space."

"You know the owner?"

"He's not...?"

Becky and Clive spoke simultaneously, the former with delight, the latter with trepidation. Chris chose to address the Captain's aborted question first.

"A vampire? No." Chris chuckled. "Nor a werewolf, for that matter."

Clive breathed a sigh of relief.

"Here you go!" Troy returned with two large bowls heaped high with icy yogurt. He barely managed to squeeze in beside Becky, sparing a mild grimace at her plate, where the sandwich still oozed sauce.

"I'll start with this one," he told Chris as if he was imparting information of great importance. "And then we can switch." He dug in, making yummy noises.

"Do you know how jealous I am?" Becky asked. "If I were to eat like that..."

"You do," Clive pointed out helpfully.

"If I were to eat like that," she repeated undaunted, "I'd gain back those forty pounds in a heartbeat."

The Captain began to speak, thought better of it, and returned to slicing up his sandwich.

"I can't believe you skipped the barbecue," Becky told Troy. "The yogurt is great, but you should try this. It's delicious. Want a bite?" She held out a fork full of sauce-drenched meat and was slightly nonplused by the look of revulsion that flickered across his face.

After years of actively disliking each other, the vampire's lover and his best friend had recently entered into a sort of armed truce. To no one's surprise, Becky was holding up her end of the bargain far better than Troy. Nevertheless, in his own way, the blond boy was trying to be cordial.

"You've got to be kid..."

"Troy." The vampire's demeanor was mild, yet his tone held a hint of warning.

"No thanks," Troy drawled with contrived politeness. "I'm fine with this." He held up his yogurt cup. "You enjoy your..." Again the flicker of distaste. "...stuff."

"So Captain," Chris said to change the subject, "I've not had the pleasure of your company for some time. What's been happening in your life?"

"Don't ask," Clive groaned. "When this..." He held up a bit of sandwich, "...is the highlight of my week..."

"If there's anything we can do," Chris' sincerity was evident, "you need only to ask."

"Christopher, you have no idea how much even the merest possibility of the two of you offering to help keeps me awake at night." Clive's sincerity was of equal gravity.

Becky chimed in. "These kidnappings are just terrible. Oh, yeah. And the parking situation for this place. But at least the city gets the revenue from the tickets and the towing."

"With seven kids missing, the only thing I'm getting is grief and more grief."

"Children?" Chris asked, his attitude suddenly far too nonchalant for the Captain's taste. "How old?"

Troy mouthed a silent "I told you so" before Chris kicked him under the table and shot him a warning glare.

Clive's eyes narrowed and he pushed his plate aside to better concentrate on the vampire.

"Why did you say it like that?"

"Like what?"

"Children," Clive mimicked.

"No reason," Chris shrugged. "I was just wondering. You hear so much about these molesters all the time. In my day, of course, it wasn't uncommon to see young people wedded and starting families by the age of fifteen. But I've seen very few modern teenagers who are mature enough to dress themselves properly without various… parts hanging out, let alone to marry. The times, they do change."

Chris continued, speaking as though he had discovered something astonishing.

"Do you know that there is now a legal age for drinking alcohol? Imagine that! When I was a boy, even the youngest stable hand would have revolted if not given his measure of beer every day. And those lads couldn't have been older than twelve or thirteen."

"These were young kids," Clive told him sternly. "Not juvenile alcoholic horseback riders. The oldest was about eleven."

"Interesting. Tell me something, Captain. Were any of them…" He smiled apologetically at Becky before finishing his question, "…rather stalwart? In girth?"

The Captain looked at him blankly.

"He wants to know if they were Fatty McFat-Fats," Troy chimed in unhelpfully.

Surprised by the question, it took a moment before the Captain could answer. "Actually, I think... er... come to think of it..."

"Ah!" The vampire looked worried. He rose from his seat. "Would you excuse me for a moment? I need to settle a mild wager with Troy. I'll be right back." He fixed his lover with a steely glare that brooked no argument. "Loose lips, Troy."

"I know! I know!" The blond mimicked zipping his mouth shut to the puzzlement of the two humans. "I'll just sit here and eat my yogurt. And flirt with that adorable Chinese guy standing over there with the green sleeveless T-shirt and the Bubble Butt of God!"

"What was that all about?" Becky demanded once Chris had managed to gain access to the EMPLOYEES ONLY inner sanctum of the yogurt shop. Try as she might, the only information she could coax from the blond were the sordid details of the paroxysms of lust he was experiencing inspired by the Asian youth, complete with some innovative ideas for the use of chopsticks. The latter mental image, she feared, might seriously hamper her enjoyment of the excellent Pineapple Chicken at Chef Ming's the next time she dined there.

Their appetites momentarily on hold, the two city officials gazed at each other with matching concern. Neither one could quite put a finger on why they found the vampire's casual comments so disquieting. In a surprisingly short period of time, the blond boy, with his South Carolina accent thickened to the consistency of Georgia Peach Pie, was hanging off the shoulder of the Chinese lad, making suitably admiring comments about how impressed he was with the size of the young man's arm muscles. Once Becky overheard Troy's topic of conversation shift onto the size of certain other portions of the youth's anatomy, by force of long habit, she was able to tune him out.

"I mentioned the kidnappings," Becky began, slowly reliving the conversation in her mind.

"And Fang Boy got super interested," Clive finished. "You don't think that he...?"

"Who? Chris?" Becky dismissed the notion with a flippant flick of her hand. "Get serious. Surely you've realized what a terrible snob he can be. He'd rather go hungry than eat something that couldn't be an Abercrombie and Fitch centerfold. Between the twinkies and the gym bunnies and the still youngish health nuts around here, this town is a smorgasbord for him. No, something else is bothering him..."

She shook her head and looked down at the vestiges of her sandwich.

"I need something sweet to cheer me up. Tangerine for you, right?"

Clive nodded and Becky went up to the counter, returning a few moments later with a small container of vibrant orange-colored frozen yogurt for the Captain and a much larger tub, the contents of which looked like Rainbow Bright had been violently ill, for herself. Spooning it into her mouth, slowly for once so that she could savor the flavor, her mind raced down several paths, each more alarming than the next. In contrast, Clive closed his lips precisely around each small spoonful, and then blotted them with a napkin each time.

Several moments passed before Chris emerged. Clive was slightly relieved to note that while the vampire looked a trifle grave, he no longer seemed as worried.

"Troy," he called.

The blond looked up and, without even a hint of shame, removed his hand from underneath the Chinese boy's shirt, where he had been ostensibly feeling the results of his "power sets."

"Heel."

With a slight scowl, Troy pecked the Asian on the cheek, confirmed that his new friend had properly punched his number into his cell phone, and promised him a demonstration of the things that could be done with half-melted yogurt before he returned to the little group at the table.

"I think it might be of immense benefit," Chris said with a deliberate calm that caused what little relief the Captain felt to flee, "if I introduced you to Razmussen."

The humans rose with questions in their eyes, yet both of them had learned that badgering Chris for answers before he was ready to give them was pointless. They followed him to the rear of the restaurant, whereupon he paused and suggested gently, "You might want to prepare yourselves."

"For what?" Becky asked.

"Anything," Chris replied blandly.

"I thought you said…" Try as he would, Clive could not quite keep the belligerence from his tone. "You said that this guy wasn't… well, you know."

"I would never lie to you, Captain. Come along now, shall we?"

CHAPTER FOUR

The vampire led the way past a small kitchen from which wafted a delicious scent of cooking meat until they came to a very large door halfway down the corridor. Chris rapped twice and, without waiting, opened it and ushered the rest through and into what turned out to be a fair-sized office.

A man with shoulders as broad as a professional wrestler was sitting behind the desk. Of indeterminate age, which could have been anywhere between thirty and sixty, his pleasantly ugly face crinkled into a welcoming smile. Ice blue eyes projected nothing but good humor and friendliness; he seemed overjoyed to have visitors. Clive's unease vanished when confronted with the genuine warmth the man exuded only to momentarily return when Razmussen stood up to shake hands.

Clive Anderson did not consider himself to be a short man, standing as he did at a hair over six feet tall, yet next to Razmussen, he felt like he should immediately go out and join the Lollipop Guild. The yogurt shop owner was easily seven feet tall and, once fully on his feet, it was clear that the comparison to a wrestler did not do him justice. Even for a giant, his muscles were so massive that they bordered on the grotesque; Clive was surprised he'd found clothing large enough to fit. On second thought, perhaps he had his wardrobe custom made by a company that manufactured camping tents, or maybe he'd simply bought a few parachutes and had them altered. Even the hand that Razmussen held out for Clive to shake was larger than most frying pans and looked like it could have twisted a cast iron one into a pretzel. Yet his grip was surprisingly and surpassingly gentle.

"Any friends of friend Christopher are friends of mine," Razmussen said, smiling. "Please, seats you will have."

The odd sentence construction indicated that the man's native tongue was not English. Becky was abundantly familiar with West Hollywood's older Russian population. While Razmussen's accent bore some similarities, there were distinct differences as well. She found herself hoping he might be German. She indulged herself in silent reminiscence of a chocolate chip and pomegranate strudel she'd once eaten and made a mental note to find out if Razmussen's culinary artistry extended to baking as well.

After the introductions were concluded and everyone was seated, the giant's smile faded into a look of subdued confusion.

"Friend Christopher tells me that my restaurant may be having the problems?" His eyes flicked back and forth between Becky and Clive, his expression clearly asking for their help. "I have all the proper permits, *ja?* The fees have all been paid? The papers all are filed in their proper little drawers?" The corners of his mouth crinkled into another little smile though his eyes remained worried. "What else must Razmussen do for making this fine city happy?"

"It's not the paperwork, Raz." Oddly, the vampire seemed hesitant. Though generally a quiet type, Chris never lacked confidence when it was needed. Both the humans knew that in his own polite way, in an instant, he could become a powerful force to be reckoned with. "It's this barbecue business."

"Yes!" the big man beamed. "You like, no? It is the most delicious meat. And the sauce!" He lowered his voice and winked slyly. "A Black Forest recipe from many ancestors past. Very..." He held an index finger half the width of a pop bottle up to his lips and made a shushing noise.

"No need to reveal secrets, Raz. Though, there are a couple of small problems that we need to discuss..."

"Very small," Troy quipped and held out his hand, palm down, at waist level. Chris glared at him and the blond immediately became absorbed with a collection of small porcelain figures that were displayed on a bookshelf.

Unfortunately, Becky was quicker on the uptake than Clive. Or maybe her long relationship with the vampire had broadened her horizons beyond the Captain's experience. She did her best to quell the not-so-random thoughts Troy's gesture had triggered. Her stomach rumbled and she felt queasy. She risked a glance at Clive but he seemed unsuspicious.

"Um, do you have a little girl's room around here?" she asked weakly.

Chris frowned. "I know it may be difficult, but please try to keep yourself under control."

"But..."

"It would be very *rude*," Chris said pointedly. "You should know by now that in our communities we value politeness and courtesy above all else. Besides, I'm not quite sure yet that..."

"But..." She felt her gorge begin to rise.

"Not now." Tersely, he cut her off.

With a gargantuan effort, the coroner managed to clench her jaw strongly enough to keep screams and other things from exploding from her mouth.

"I don't understand," Clive was mildly confused.

"Nor I, friend Captain," Razmussen agreed. "Is problem with yogurt? Both goat milk and yak milk are first pasteurized as your laws instruct." The big man's sunny disposition vanished and he suddenly looked like he was about to cry. "I am taking great care to do no things wrong."

"It's not the milk, Raz," Chris said, doing his best to ease the big man's mind. "But it might be the meat."

"Finest quality!" Razmussen's happiness was restored. "Young, tender! Handpicked!"

"And that would be the problem," Chris sighed with as much sympathy as he could. "This is America, Raz. We're living in the twentieth century..."

"Twenty-first," Becky corrected.

The vampire waved away her comment as if the specifics were

unimportant to him. "You can't just go around picking up..." He paused and looked sideways at Clive, hoping to gauge what his reaction would be. "...meat from the streets."

"Why not?" Razmussen was baffled. "Would just go to waste otherwise."

"Wait a minute..." Clive leaned forward, one hand gripping the arm of his chair, the other clutching instinctively at his belly. "You're not suggesting... What waste? ...This guy isn't..." He looked from Chris to Razmussen and back again, shocked. "He's not using *road kill* in the barbecue is he?" A huge belch rose to the back of his throat and he swallowed it back down, fearful of the mess he might make if it escaped.

"Not exactly road kill, Captain."

A look of unadulterated horror blossomed on the Captain's face. He bolted from his chair, frantic.

With the inbred grace of generations of Southern hostesses, Troy already held the office door open for him. "It's down the hall and to the left," he said.

Chris sighed. "I suppose you had better go too, Becky."

"Thanks," she managed to gasp before she also ran pell-mell for the bathroom.

CHAPTER FIVE

"Humans!" Razmussen said, shaking his head with something akin to bemused affection.

"Their ways are not our ways," Chris confirmed, companionably. "But, my friend, I'm afraid you may have made a terrible mistake."

"Can be fixed?" he asked with deep concern.

"We'll have to hope so, won't we? In the meantime, let's just enjoy each other's company and not worry about it until they return."

For several minutes, they sat swapping reminiscences of old acquaintances and chuckling over incidents from their mutual pasts. Eventually, Becky staggered back into the office and collapsed into a chair. A moment or so later, Clive followed, his brow dotted with perspiration, his face wan and the muscles of his jaw tight.

"Mister Razmussen," he announced with stiff formality, "you're under arrest. You have the right to…"

"Not so fast, Captain," Chris chided mildly.

"*You* do *not* tell *me* how to enforce the law in this city, Christopher." He barely managed to restrain his fury.

"I would never presume, Captain," the vampire replied, holding up his hands, palms out, in mock surrender. "There are, however, a few facts you may wish to consider before continuing."

"Like what? Is this bozo going to deny that he killed seven innocent children and *served* them to his customers?"

"You see?" Razmussen enthused. "Very young! Very fresh! Only the best for this new country I am coming to!"

"I don't think denial is a part of this."

Clive could not understand how the vampire could remain so calm.

"I think this is about understanding. And tolerance," Chris finished pointedly. "After all, the city of West Hollywood was founded on tolerance. Tolerance for gay people, for recent immigrants, for people whose rights were abused elsewhere, even tolerance for personal eccentricity no matter how odd. Tolerance."

"Tolerance? Are you out of your tree?" The Captain's look of horrified disbelief would have been comical but for its intensity. "Tolerance is when there's a pre-op transsexual who forgot to shave her beard sitting behind your chiropractor's reception desk. Tolerance is letting a Farmer's Market vendor sell durians to his Indonesian customers so long as he puts his stall at the far end of the parking lot where no one else has to smell them. Tolerance is shutting your mouth when Pam Burman walks around wearing something that looks like a trainload of kaleidoscopes smashed into an eighteen-wheeler full of Fruit Loops. *This* is not tolerance!"

He drew his gun and leveled it.

"Friend Christopher?" Rather than being frightened by the pistol pointed at his chest, Razmussen seemed to be struggling not to show that Clive had hurt his feelings by his violent reaction.

"You cannot punish a person simply for being what they are," Chris chided gently.

"I think," Becky managed to croak past a throat sore from vomiting, "that we'd better hear him out, Clive."

"Hear him out?" As far as Clive was concerned, everyone in the room seemed to have gone completely crazy with the sole exception of Troy, which was problematic in and of itself. "Fine!" he spat. He lowered the gun but didn't holster it. "Just what the hell *is* your friend here? The one that I can't blame for being what he is?"

"Is okay?" the big man asked Chris, doubtfully.

"I don't see that you've got much of a choice, Raz. Don't worry. I'll protect you."

"You'll do nothing of the kind..." Clive said heatedly. "If this man is a murderer... a child murderer no less..."

"I am ogre."

CHAPTER SIX

Razmussen made the announcement as if it was no big deal, as if it were so self-evident that he could not understand why it would even be an issue for anyone.

The Captain's words died in his mouth and the entire room suddenly grew deathly silent.

"Well," Troy said brightly. "That's certainly one way to kill a conversation." He cast a disparaging glance at Razmussen. "Remind me never to let you escort me to any of the fashionable parties."

"That explains the missing kids," Becky said in a weak whisper. "Tell me," she looked at Chris with confusion swimming in her eyes. "Isn't there supposed to be something about a bridge?"

"That would be a troll," he chuckled. "Razmussen is an ogre."

"A child killer."

"True, Captain," he agreed solemnly. "But that's what he *is*. You can't blame him for it."

"I can sure as hell blame him for serving a Little League team to half the celebrities in Hollywood!"

"I'm sure it's not as bad as all that," Chris assured him. His expression was serious but amusement danced in his eyes. "Seven children would hardly be enough to feed that many."

"You seem to think this is funny. I don't. I find nothing funny about slaughtering innocent children and..."

"Oh no!" Razmussen held up his hands and waved them frantically to attract the Captain's attention. "Not innocent! *Never* innocent!" he cried with dismay.

"What are you talking about?" Clive challenged.

The ogre hastened to explain. "Is law of all ogres. God created to punish bad children. Evil children. Innocent children not allowed since Edict of Krampus."

"What the hell is a Krampus?"

"He's a who, not a what," Chris told him. "Technically, he's a demon but he's often mistaken for an ogre because he hangs out with them. About three hundred years ago, he stopped trying to set the record straight and started going along with it. But that's another story."

"My head hurts," Becky said in a somewhat dazed voice. "My stomach wants to leave my body through my nose and my head is spinning. I feel like I'm going to pass out."

"Breathe," Troy suggested helpfully. "And remember that a proper young lady should always carry a fan. I'd lend you one of mine but in these pants..."

He whirled around to model the trousers. Becky noticed that a small patch had been sewn on just above the buttocks. Outlined in tiny rhinestones, it bore the legend REAR ENTRANCE.

"The pockets are too small. You want to be able to sort of flutter it in front of your face." He demonstrated with an imaginary fan. "Like this. We used to call it an attack of the vapors. The fan doesn't do much for the dizziness, but the second they see it, all the handsome young gentleman come running to catch you before you fall."

His eyes, misty with the memory of at least several such incidents, abruptly cleared when an unpalatable thought struck him.

"You'll want to take a gander around you first, though," he advised. "To make sure there actually *are* some handsome young gentlemen in the area. Otherwise, you might end up with a fat, disgusting old guy with pimples waving smelling salts under your nose." He shuddered. "What's the point of having an attack of the vapors if it's going to be wasted on some fat, disgusting old guy waving..."

"That will be quite enough, Monkey," Chris chided mildly. "The adults are talking."

"It doesn't matter if the children were good or bad." Clive was adamant about this. Not even Troy's chatter had defused his commitment to shooting the ogre where he stood. The gun barrel rose to point at Razmussen's chest once again.

"This guy isn't Santa Claus. If a child misbehaves, you put coal in his stocking, you don't roast him over an open fire."

"Roast?" The ogre seemed horrified at the very notion. "No! No!" He wrung his hands. "Slow braise! Long cooking helps develop flavor." Earnestly, he delivered a bit of culinary advice. "Using beer, not hard spirits. Mixing in whole herbs, delicately crushed to release flavor. Is old family recipe as well." Again, he brought his huge fin-ger to his lips to indicate that what he had confided was a closely held secret.

Chris reached out and gently wrapped his hand around Clive's wrist, careful not to startle him into pulling the trigger. He applied a slight downward pressure that slowly increased as he spoke.

"You may wish to know, Captain, that there are only three things that a bullet will do. Since it cannot penetrate his flesh, it will un-doubtedly ricochet and ruin Razmussen's lovely wallpaper, which would be a shame. Second, it could potentially go astray and injure one of the two of you. And finally, it might hurt Troy. While I con-sider you both good friends and I would greatly regret the former, I will not tolerate even the slightest possibility of the latter. Therefore, I must insist..." His voice hardened while still remaining fairly con-versational. "...that you put the gun away."

"Bull," Clive muttered. "It may not kill him. But I've seen you get shot, Christopher. It'll hurt him long enough for..."

The vampire smiled again. "We are not all alike, Captain. As you should know by now."

"Do what he says, Clive. If Mister Razmussen here is an ogre..." Becky frowned with the strain of trying to recall something from her distant past. "I read something once..." Her voice trailed off while she struggled to remember something. "With ogres," she exclaimed, proud of herself for remembering, "you need a goat!"

"That would be trolls as well," Chris told her. His focus returned to the Captain. "What harm can a few minutes of listening do? It's not like Raz is unwilling to cooperate."

"What if he tries to escape?"

Chris looked at him pityingly. "If Razmussen wished to leave, nothing short of your ex-Governor Schwartzenegger in a Teflon suit could stop him. Even then, I don't think I'd care to lay odds on it. I know this is difficult for you considering what you may have just eaten..."

"Don't remind me." He looked very ill once again.

"...Please let's all be civilized about this, shall we? There will always be time for shooting off guns and breaking down walls later."

Though his expression remained neutral, Chris maintained un-wavering eye contact with the Captain until he was certain that the gun was well and truly re-holstered. Satisfied, he smiled encouragement at Razmussen. "Raz, go ahead and tell the Captain about the bad children."

Becky envied the vampire's calm. Then again, she figured that to a guy who slurped up lunch from people's necks, maybe chowing down on a preschooler or two wasn't such a big deal.

"Was only some bad," Razmussen hastened to correct. "Some already evil, some only bad. Bad would become evil, in time. But not yet." One huge fist pounded his massive chest. "Razmussen obeys laws! Besides...," He made a grimace and worked his thick tongue against his soft palate in an unattractive motion that suggested he'd just eaten something foul and was trying to work the taste out of his mouth. "Good children often too bland. Texture can be mushy."

"Oh. Well. If *that's* the case, Razmussen now has my complete sympathy." Clive's sarcasm was abundant.

"First child was girl child. Evil. Hurt many small animals. Broke wings of birds. Hit kitten with hammer. Begins to looking at knives. Very dangerous. Second was brother and sister. Also evil. Together, used pillow on baby. Baby die," he said mournfully. Then, he added with some regret. "Baby was good baby. Not proper to eat."

"Are you telling me...?"

"Let him finish, Clive."

The ogre's story tickled Becky's interest. Several months ago she'd performed an autopsy on the Guillerman infant. Although everything *seemed* to point to a garden-variety crib death, there had been something about the child's demise that troubled her. Lacking any evidence other than her instincts, and not wanting to add to the grief of the already distraught parents, she'd reluctantly certified the death as natural. In retrospect, perhaps she'd been too hasty, especially as she now recalled that the Guillermans had other children as well. A slightly older set of fraternal twins.

"Small boy set grandmother on fire. Angry not allowed to eat candy. Grandmother live, but boy liking fire now."

Clive inhaled sharply and Becky was quick to pounce.

"What is it?"

"Back in March, Fred Delaney called me in on a possible arson over on Vista Street."

"Fred sees arson everywhere. He probably dreams about it." The West Hollywood Fire Chief was known for his eccentricity where fire was concerned. At certain levels in the halls of city government, it had long been speculated that had Delaney not gone into fire abatement, he might have ended up behind bars as an arsonist himself.

"This was different. We knew the old lady had been deliberately set on fire. But no one was talking. Eventually, we had to let it go. If the kid did it, it explains why the family was so closed mouth."

Razmussen was nodding his head enthusiastically, looking very much like a half-scale model of a King Kong bobble head, albeit with slightly less hair.

"Yes! Was most evil of all children. Becomes angry. Hurts. No love in heart."

"There are seven missing, Mister Razmussen. That leaves three more." Evidently, Becky had been keeping count.

"Ah yes! Two children are… what is word for people who make good business? People like Razmussen who create business?" He looked helplessly at the vampire and mouthed a garbled sound reminiscent of a water buffalo being strangled.

"Entrepreneur?" Chris translated.

"Yes! Was entrepreneurs. But not making good business. Making bad business." He shook his head, deeply disturbed by what he knew. "Selling of powder and pills to playmates from school."

"Kiddy drug dealers?"

Clive motioned her to be quiet. "The playground in Plummer Park. There were some problems reported. They're using kids now. If we catch 'em, they go to juvenile hall until they're eighteen. The big wigs figure it's safer than an adult risking fifteen-to-thirty for dealing himself." The Captain was caught by what the ogre was saying and seemed, at least for the moment, far less likely to start aiming and pulling triggers. "Go on."

"Last child… Last child…" Razmussen suddenly seemed uncomfortable.

"The last child was not, perhaps, strictly a bad child, was it?" Chris suggested gently. "No need to start playing cowboy again, Captain. If I'm correct, Razmussen is feeling bad enough about it already. Isn't that right, Raz?"

The ogre sighed heavily, the force of his exhalation strong enough to reach across the room and rattle the collection of incongruously delicate porcelain figures that Troy had been admiring earlier.

"Is difficult," he admitted. "Was partly bad child. Could be evil child in future. But also was child with very ill mind." He tapped his temple with a forefinger. "Was sad. Very sad. Did nasty, dirty things with other children. Not nice things. Also with small fluffy dog."

Becky opened her mouth to say something. Seeing the conflicted look on Clive Anderson's face, she thought better of it and remained silent. She'd already reached her own decision; Clive needed to work his out for himself.

"This does not," he finally said slowly and softly, "excuse the murder of seven children." He glared at Razmussen with uncertainty. "Nor the fact that you've made Becky and me unsuspecting cannibals."

"Cannibals?" Razmussen looked confused for a long moment before understanding dawned. He threw back his head and gave vent to a loud bray of laughter. "Friends of friend Christopher think that they have eaten…?"

He shook so hard when he laughed that Becky expected the vibrations to dislodge chunks of plaster from the ceiling.

"What's so damned funny?" Clive's face was purpled with anger.

The vampire touched his arm to urge caution, but Clive abruptly shook his hand away.

"You think..." The giant gasped, his eyes shining with mirth. "You are thinking you have eaten child meat?"

"That *is* what we're talking about, isn't it?" Clive snapped.

"Oh dear. Is very funny." Razmussen lifted his shirttail to wipe tears from his eyes, incidentally baring a swathe of heavily muscled yet unbelievably hairy stomach in the process. "Friends of friend Christopher are important people but..." He paused and fumbled to choose words least likely to offend his guests. "You order from counter, yes?"

"Yes," Becky confirmed.

"You are expecting child meat barbecue for price of sandwich ordered at *counter*?" The chuckling started anew. "Child meat is *delicacy*," he explained, highly amused at their temerity. "A child meat sandwich? For eleven dollars and forty-nine cents?" He managed, with great effort, not to burst into laughter again.

"The people of this country are very naive. Eleven dollars forty-nine cents is good price for pork or beef. Not bad for yak neither," he mused. "Must consider raising price of yak barbecue. Is expensive to import, you know."

"Do you mean...?" The relief on Clive's face was palpable.

"Child meat is for good customers only," Razmussen assured

them. "Excellent customers. Customers who will like to pay large prices for small sandwiches."

"Um, Mister Razmussen?" Becky asked tentatively. "Who exactly ate these child meat sandwiches?"

"No one eat yet," he said, as if surprised that she had to ask. "I had small taste. To correct spices. Must hang carcass for several weeks for flavor to develop. Marinate in seasonings for many days. Then pounding into wafer thin steaks before cooking at very low temper..."

"All righty then!" Becky cut him off with forced cheeriness, neatly avoiding having to hear any more details of the proper methods of preparing pre-adolescent brisket. "So who are the lucky diners who will be tasting this marvelous meal you're preparing?"

The ogre's massive chest puffed with pride and incidentally gained another foot and a half in circumference. "Is exclusively reserved for Academy Award-winning director Monte Wilbursen. Having party next week to celebrate new film opening to big office boxes! One hundred six million boxes in first weekend!" Razmussen looked momentarily impressed before giving in to slight confusion. "What is use for so many boxes? Is mailing many things?"

"I'll make some calls and see what I can do about heading off this disaster at the pass," Becky told Clive, *sotto voce*. She noted Clive's look of grim determination. "Don't you even *think* of getting the Health Department in here! We can handle this ourselves."

"But..."

"You can't close a man down for serving a helping or two of yak, Captain."

"That's not the point, Christopher! And you know it! This man killed..."

"Seven budding psychopaths from what I heard. Though if I had to be truthful, I'd venture that Raz may have gone a smidgen overboard with the two wanna-be drug dealers. Would it be too much for you to cut him a break, Captain? After all, making a mistake is only..." His ironic smile showed a goodly portion of fang this time. "...human."

"I can't cover up something like..."

"Yes, you can," Becky told him firmly. "We've done it before. And, unfortunately," she added with a heavy sigh, "we'll probably end up doing it again. There are consequences, though." She hauled herself to her feet and addressed the large man with adamant gravity. "Mister Razmussen, if you are going to continue operating your business in West Hollywood, we have a couple of conditions. Are you listening carefully?"

The ogre nodded.

"No more serving children. Not as counter sandwiches *or* to your good customers. Are we clear about that?"

"But..." The ogre seemed baffled by the demand.

"It's a different world than the one we used to know, Raz. Sometimes, in order to survive in it, you have to make concessions. Besides, she's only worried about you serving them to humans; she said nothing about eating them yourself so..."

"*That* was my next issue!" she hastily interrupted.

"Becky, you cannot expect the man to..."

"He's not a man and yes I can."

"Can we compromise?" Chris turned on the charm and, not for the first time, Becky's stubbornness gave way before it. "If I can come up with a solution that's more… palatable?"

"What did you have in mind?"

"My understanding," Chris began, "is that no one particularly minds the actual *eating* of children, which his nature requires, by the way. It's the *killing* that you all object to."

Becky ventured a tentative nod.

"Excellent!" The vampire rubbed his hands together happily. "You've got a freezer here, right, Raz? I'll get in touch with some friends and take care of everything."

"I know I'm gonna regret asking this. What the heck are you talking about?"

"Imports," Chris told her. "We may have some small inconvenience getting everything through customs. Fortunately, I have a few old friends who have influence with the harbor inspectors down in Long Beach. They'll handle the details."

"Christopher," Clive began with long-suffering patience. "It doesn't matter whether they're from Sherman Oaks or imported from Borneo. Mister Razmussen can*not* blithely continue slaughtering children willy nilly and baking them into meat pies."

"Barbecue."

Clive ignored the ogre's correction, his jaw set against any of the vampire's objections.

"Of course not, Captain! That would be silly," he beamed. "They'll be flash frozen after they've died on their own."

"What?"

"Oh, I know it's not a hundred percent perfect solution. We'll certainly tell our sources that we'd prefer it if the...er ... product not be quite so fresh. You're not particular about the age of the corpse, are you, Raz? Not if it means being able to continue living here without attracting attention?"

The ogre shrugged. "Will do what must be done," he conceded, but he didn't appear happy about it.

"You're going to be shipping dead, frozen children into Long Beach..."

"For Razmussen's personal consumption only, right, Raz? No more human barbecue."

"No yak either, while we're at it," Clive said, dully. He seemed more resigned to the idea. "I'm pretty sure it's not legal to serve unless he gets the proper health permits from the county. And let's try to do something about the parking situation around here while we're at it, can we?"

"First things first, Captain," Chris said. "First things first. Now that we've conquered the barbecue problem..." He stood up. "Raz, might I trouble you to pack up a few quarts of my special blend of yogurt to go?"

"Coconut, too?" Troy begged. "And maybe some of that yummy kind that tastes like orange pop?"

"Just put it on my tab."

"Your... *special* blend?" Clive swallowed, his throat suddenly dry.

"Oh please, Captain," Chris told him, airily waving away his concerns. "Let's not create yet another issue where none exists, shall we?"

This time when he smiled, Clive had no problem seeing the entirety of his incisors, right down to the sharply pointed tips.

"After all," the vampire reminded him, not unkindly. "It's all about tolerance, isn't it?"

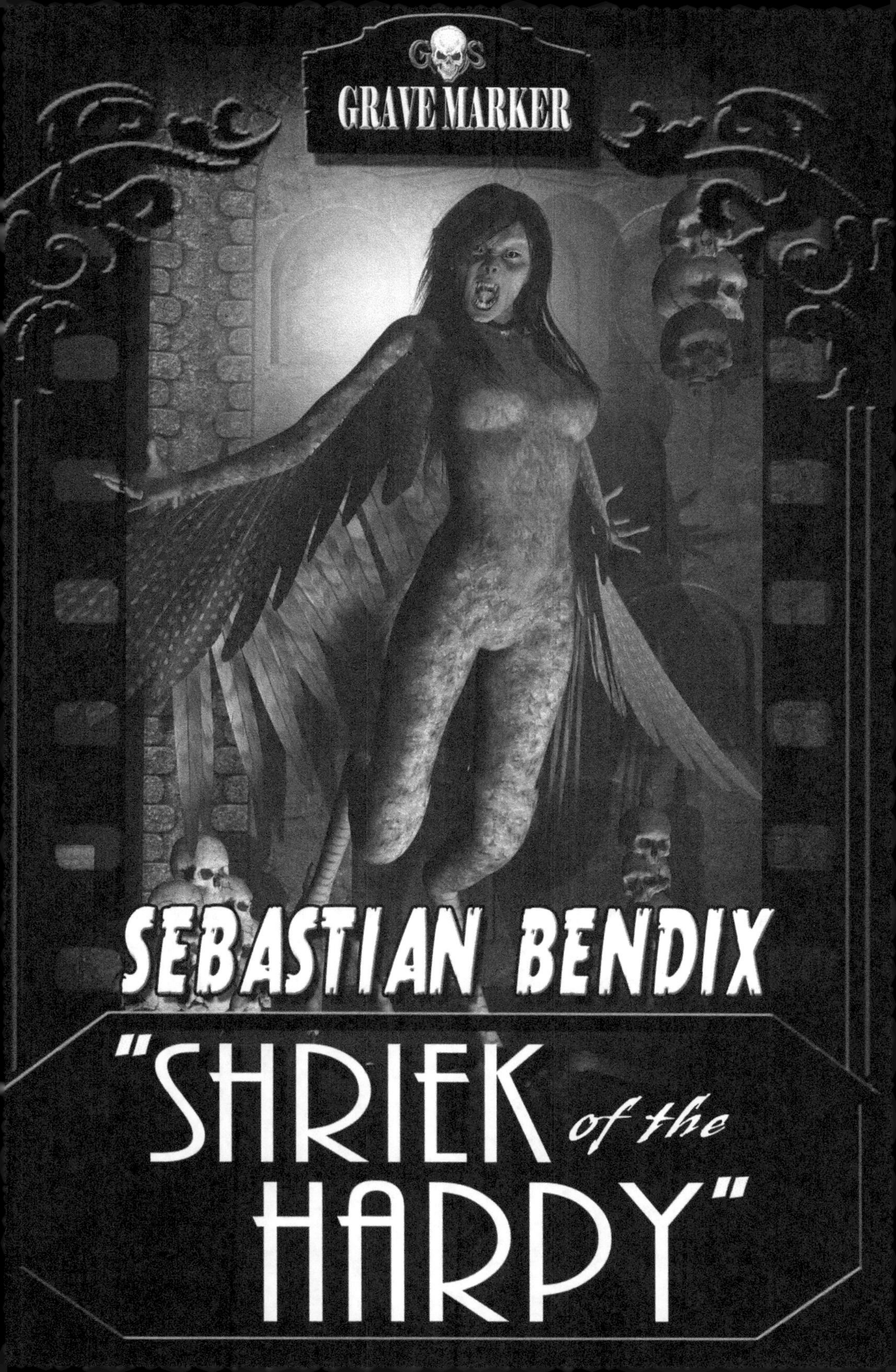
GRAVE MARKER
SEBASTIAN BENDIX
"SHRIEK of the HARPY"

OPENING CREDITS

NOV. 8TH

OBJECTIVE ACHIEVED!!!

Guys — it finally happened! I GOT THE JOB!! Yes, your intrepid blogger Muriel Sharpe has FINALLY landed her dream gig as a film archivist. I'M SO EXCITED!!! It took me 4 years of undergrad and 2 post, but I am at last ready to make my big screen debut! And by that I mean getting down with some SERIOUS ARCHIVING and film restoration!

But of course, it wouldn't be my life if there wasn't a cloud to the silver lining. As it turns out, I'm not super crazy about my bosses. First of all, their names are Kurt and Kitt? Are you fucking kidding me? KURT and KITT??? Did they like, apply for their positions at the same time wearing matching outfits? At first I thought they HAD to be a couple, but nope, not even dating. They're both annoyingly attracttive, too, perfect, skinny, and blonde. Totally LA... and we know how much I LOVE that. Seriously, if I could live somewhere else, I would be out of here in a heartbeat. I am so OVER this town. But here is where I need to be to do what I love, so Kurt and Kitt are what I have to deal with. At least for the time being.

Oh, and one thing, OF COURSE, Kurt is a TOTAL CHAU-VINIST. Even after I got the job he kept questioning me about my qualifications and I'm like, hello! EIGHT YEARS OF SCHOOL!! But no, he keeps going on and on about "practical experience" as if I'm some ditzy girl who doesn't know how to handle a film print or something. And I mean, yeah, I haven't done a TON of print han-dling, but I've spent a lot of time with Gina in the booth of the Crescent and I think that with my EDUCATION the point should be moot. But it's not, because I am a woman. And Kitt, instead of backing up a sister, just stands there nodding to everything Kurt says like some sort of Barbie automaton. WHATEVER. I'll make the best of it, but I got a misogynist vibe there, BIG TIME.

Anyway, heading into the office to talk about my first real assign-ment! Later for now!

CHAPTER ONE

The Downtown Nickelodeon, known to local cinephiles as "The Old Nick", was tucked in between a Mexican grocer and a used stereo store on 8th Street in the heart of downtown Los Angeles. The once-garish marquee had been torn down long ago, but the greasy window of the boarded-up ticket booth was still visible to the keen-eyed observer. Muriel had to use Google maps to find it, a fact that gave her a twinge of shame as she prided herself on knowing the locations of all the old Hollywood movie houses. Even in its heyday, the Nick was a lesser-frequented theater, mostly a second-run venue, so Muriel felt she could afford a little slack. Besides, as exciting as this assignment was, it seemed more janitorial than archive related, and Muriel was a little off put that this dingy rung on the ladder was where she was expected to start. *I suppose I should be grateful that I landed the job,* Muriel told herself. But thinking it was one thing; believing was another matter entirely.

Standing at the chained and padlocked front doors, she rooted through her fully stuffed backpack for the keys. Past a bag of Skittles and a travel bottle of Aussie hairspray she found them, twisted and stuck in the tines of one of her roller-style hairbrushes. Muriel sighed as she pulled the keys loose, carrying the weight of the world on her mannish shoulders. Adding injury to insult, the sky began to drizzle, dampening her hair into a flat, frizzy mop. *California rain is a rare and bad omen*, thought Muriel glumly. *Why did things always have to be so hard?*

But Muriel's soggy spirits were lifted as she took in the wonderful, decaying lobby with its grand staircase and tall proscenium archways. The velvet curtains were tattered and moth-eaten and the fixtures — no doubt scavenged for scrap — were long gone, but the theater held on proudly to its old-world glamor, even under an apocalyptic layer of dust. A toppled stanchion still clung to a coiled, rotted rope, and the ruin of a concession booth promised popcorn, soda, and candy that had long been consumed. Stepping fully into the lobby, Muriel's footfalls echoed off of the chipped marble floor, invoking the ghost heels of movie-goers past, and she found herself swept up in a wave of nostalgia for a time she had never lived. To a film preservationist, this was not an uncommon sensation, but here, in this once-vital house of cinema, the feelings were amplified tenfold, redefined with crystalline clarity.

The focal point of the lobby was a large marble fountain that stood at the apex of the room like a holy altar. It was cracked and crumbling and hadn't held water since the sixties at the latest, but it still had the power to command the viewer's attention. As a centerpiece for a movie theater lobby, it was quite unusual, both garish and beautiful, and Muriel approached it with a mixed appreciation. It was a multi-layered construction; a medium-size pool hung suspended by a column above a larger ground-level pool, the sea-shell sculpt of both suggesting an odd mid-century fusion of nautical and art nouveau. Draped upon the column, in a spiraling, heavenward pattern, were winged cherubs, or, upon closer inspection, angels. Even as an agnostically raised girl, Muriel had an affinity for angels, viewing them as symbols of feminine power and strength. It gave her some comfort to know they were there, keeping her in sight as she ventured into the darkened recesses of the theater.

It took her a few minutes to find the breaker room, despite the fact that Kurt had explained to her in detail where it was located, to the far left of the dilapidated concession booth. It was dark and cluttered and she needed her phone's flashlight to find her way, but when she flipped on the breakers, the theater was rewarded with welcoming light. Some bulbs popped from the strain of being suddenly revived, but the ones that survived gave off a hazily sufficient illumination. Apparently Kitt was good enough at her job to put in the necessary call to the power company and not leave her new employee fumbling in the dark. "Hooray for small miracles," Muriel remarked aloud, giving herself the tiniest of chuckles.

Beyond the lobby were the doors leading to the main auditorium, and stepping through them, Muriel was once again transported across time. The three-story screen was yellowed and torn in several places, but it put to shame most found in modern megaplexes outside of the ones made to IMAX specifications. One could easily imagine taking in a matinee show of *Lawrence of Arabia* here during its initial run and getting entirely lost in the projected vistas, overwhelmed by the sheer scope of the all-encompassing anamorphic image. The seats, still arranged in their three-section pattern, had gone to seed long ago and the room hung thick with the smell of mildew, rot, and the specter of cigarettes smoked long ago. But it wouldn't have stopped Muriel from plopping down and digging into a bucket of popcorn had some time-traveling projectionist started running a freshly struck print of *Double Indemnity* or, even better, *Touch of Evil*.

Above and to the back was a grand balcony, the kind you didn't see any more in movie theaters, and Muriel could almost make out the silhouettes of couples necking in the shadowy back rows. Ten feet or so above the balcony was the dusty window of the projection booth, looking out over the auditorium like a giant's cataracted pupil. There lay Muriel's destination, but down here, in the safety of the aisles, it didn't look like a very inviting place. The blackness within had the stillness of a crypt and Muriel could not shake the feeling that whatever slept up there was something that was best left undisturbed.

But it was her job to venture into that crypt, so after lingering a bit in the auditorium's splendor, she summoned her courage, slipped the key into the lock of the projection booth door, and entered to a stale gust of air. The light from the hall barely cut into the gloom, so Muriel fumbled along the wall for a light switch, at last finding one and flicking it on. She needed a moment to take in what lay there before her. The room was dusty and stale and didn't appear to have been used in many a decade, but this was all to be expected. The cutting table had fallen to termites and years of neglect, leaving one of the legs snapped and the table top tipped over at an angle. The splicing equipment sat rusting on the floor with scraps of old leader littered about it like scattered petals. But the projectors, twin hulks of iron, glass, and steel, looked shockingly intact. Muriel found herself running a hand along their smooth, pleasing forms the way someone might do to a thoroughbred pony or a finely restored vintage car. There was sensuality to their construction that was lost in modern equipment, a craftsmanship that had fallen by the wayside for the sake of efficiency and progress. It saddened Muriel to see them so neglected, and even though it had not been suggested or even implied in her duties, she was tempted to fire up the twin workhorses to see if they still ran.

What *was* implicit in her duties was to inventory the moldy boxes that had been stored in the booth for the better part of the century and see if they held any lost prints. Stacks upon stacks of boxes lined the walls, sagging under the weight of the years and leaning together like old people needing the other's support. They reeked of mildew and rot and their corners were ragged and rat-chewed, but still they held a certain sad air of dignity.

"Might as well get started," Muriel sighed to herself. But in truth, she was thrilled as she wandered into the stacks and picked a box from the top layer, careful that it wouldn't upset the others. She set it down on the floor and tore open the moldy boxtop, an eager child digging into a Christmas present.

Her nose and throat were immediately greeted by a blast of noxious fumes — the reek of photo chemicals that were far past their expiration date. But the unpleasant odor was a small price to pay for the glory that lay within. Stacked neatly in the box were circular tins — the kind used to house prints in the old days. She felt the same sort of thrill an archeologist might feel uncovering relics that had been buried for almost a century.

INTERMISSION

NOV. 11TH

GOLDEN AGE HOLLYWOOD GLAMOUR AT THE OLD
NICK

One word ... AMAZING!!! My first day working at the Old
Nick was everything I could have dreamed! I mean, at first I was a
little skeezed out being by myself in such a huge abandoned building,
but after a few minutes I took to the place like a fish to water! Looks
like this old gal (not really, I just turned 35 ... still young!) was born
to be a world-class film archivist. As if there was ever any doubt!

So as it turns out, I guess my bosses aren't TOTALLY CLUE-
LESS, though I seriously don't think they know what they have with
the prints I found in the projection booth. In truth, I don't know
what we have either, but you bet your butt I aim to find out! It's not
going to be easy — the masking tape labels are worn and unreadable
so I'm going to have to get my hands dirty and look at the prints with
my own equipment, something that I'm not really supposed to be doing. But screw that! I'm not going to let those Ken and Barbie robots
get the credit for finding some lost classic! I didn't tell either of them
about my blog, but I know I can trust you guys. That said, mum's the

word. First rule of fight club, don't let the cat out of the bag, etc...

ANYWAY, more will be revealed when I go back there tomorrow. If it weren't for the fact that I need to shower and get online to post, I would probably sleep there. I have the feeling that I'll be pulling an all-nighter one of these days, or nights rather! ;)

CHAPTER TWO

The following morning Muriel arrived at the Old Nick early, pausing only a moment to admire her fountain angels before heading directly into the booth. Any reservations she had from the previous day were gone; now the theater was an old and trusted friend and she was its loyal caretaker. She loved its peeling walls and threadbare carpets, and if she had been a woman of wealth, she would have bought the place herself and restored it to its former glory. Alas, all of her trust fund had gone to college, and film archiving, while spiritually rewarding, was not likely to make her rich. It was a sad feeling to know that her time here was brief, that the Nick would soon be gone entirely. But Muriel was no stranger to sad feelings, so she pushed them aside and set about getting to work.

With a little creative — re: jury-rigged — re-construction, Muriel was able to get the old splicing table reasonably stabilized and quickly set up her own equipment. Less than a half an hour later she was holding her first piece of celluloid under the looking glass and parsing through clues as to its title of origin. She identified it as a print of *To*

Kill A Mockingbird, and while this was a film Muriel quite enjoyed, it was a well-documented title and something most students had seen by their first year of American lit. Putting it aside, she dug into another box, then another, opening tin after tin, her spirits falling with every unremarkable find. *Sunset Boulevard, The Asphalt Jungle, Cat People* — all wonderful films but all easily found on DVD, Blu-Ray, or TCM on any given night. As the morning wore on, Muriel began to suspect that she would not uncover any lost relics in this dreary acquisition, and the feeling that her talents were being wasted re-surfaced like a badly digested meal.

After lunch Muriel resolved to remain optimistic and shifted her focus to a stack of boxes that sat in the corner, looking somehow moldier and more pathetic than the ones she had opened already. Opening the first of the boxes, she was hit with a gust so foul that she could only assume something had crawled into the packaging and died, likely a mouse or small rat. She shifted the tins around, checking the corners, and was happy to find the box free of rotting animal corpses. But that horrible smell had to be something, and she wondered if it would be wise to invest in a breathing mask, or to stop the work altogether. Cancer was not high on her list of wants, but the fear of it was not enough to keep her from cracking the first of the tins. Looking down at the magic that was coiled within dissipated her apprehension along with the fumes.

Just by eyeballing the way the print had been stored, Muriel was certain that she was looking at something from the 1930s or earlier, significantly increasing the odds that she had unearthed something that had been lost in the annals of time. As with the other reels, the masking tape labels were degraded and illegible, so the only way to identify the print was by putting it onto her table and under the glass, which is exactly what she did. There, magnified in vibrant, full-frame black and white, were images that Muriel had seen only in film history documentaries and reference books. She scrolled the reel towards the leader, heart leaping as she scanned the frames for the title card. When she found it, she had to steady herself from fainting.

Looking back up at her in elegant script were the words "Blind Courtesy".

Blind Courtesy was a drama from 1931 that had been directed by British auteur Lyle Abernathy, who would only go on to direct two more Hollywood films before returning to his home country to care for his infirmed and ailing mother. The film's primary claim to fame was that it starred silent era ingénue Delia Whitmore in her first sound role, and critics had responded so unkindly to her deep, manly voice that the tortured actress hung herself a mere month after the picture ended its first and only theatrical run. In a sad twist of irony, Whitmore was nominated for a posthumous Oscar, but lost to Helen Hayes and *The Sins of Madelon Claudet*. Even in death, poor Delia could find no validation — a feeling to which Muriel, seeking validation herself, could relate.

Despite the apologetic nomination, the film was a box office flop, and after a fire on the Warner Brothers lot in 1940, it was assumed that all known prints of the film had been destroyed. But here Muriel was looking at one, crisp and clean as it was on the day of its eighty-year-old debut. How it had remained here undiscovered was a mystery, but the answer, likely a matter of simple neglect, was irrelevant. Now there was the only the question of what to do next.

Muriel knew what her type-A bosses Kurt and Kitt would want her to do. They would want her to follow protocol, to re-box the print immediately and deliver it straight to the home office. From there it would be shipped back to the studio, shelved indefinitely unless some bean-counting executive deemed it profitable to shit out the film in a half-assed streaming format. And that was if things went well. More likely was that *Blind Courtesy* would remain in the dustbins of obscurity and no one, Muriel included, would ever have the pleasure of seeing it. The thought of this heinous injustice, this crime against cinema, was too much for Muriel to rightfully bear. It went against everything she believed in as an archivist, and as a film lover.

Screw Kurt and Kitt, screw their protocols, and screw the studio! Muriel had to experience this lost treasure as it had been intended — on the silver screen. And she was willing to risk it all — her career, her future, everything — for the privilege.

She looked to the twin projectors, standing tall like iron sentinels. There was something about them, some quiet, ancient wisdom that made Muriel question what she was about to do on a deep, preternatural level. But the lure of *Blind Courtesy* was impossible for her to resist, so she returned her focus to the table and carefully set about assembling the five-reel print. An hour later, her trembling hands threaded the lead of reel one into the gate and the film was ready to be viewed for the first time in many decades.

With the flick of a switch, the projectors rattled to life, and for a horrified moment, Muriel was sure that they were going to seize up and mangle the print. But the gate fluttered gently, like the soft beating of a moth's wings, and the strip ran through unfettered. The twin bulbs lit with a soft glow, and down in the darkened auditorium, images once lost in time were recalled from the ether like welcome ghosts. Muriel could hear the scuffling of shoes and the rustle of fingers in popcorn boxes echoing through time, and she wanted so desperately to join them.

To hell with it, Muriel thought. *If I am going to risk my job by running this, why should I stay up here for the entire screening?* Of course, the responsible thing to do would be to remain in the booth and monitor the projectors, but Muriel had passed responsible a ways back and gone barreling straight on to reckless. To come this far only to be denied the experience of watching the film in a darkened theater, well, that would just be stupid. And if there was one thing that Muriel Sharpe couldn't stand, it was thinking of herself of as stupid.

So it was decided. She checked the gates one last time, and satisfied that all was working properly, she went downstairs to take in a private, once-in-a-lifetime screening of *Blind Courtesy*. Her only regret was that she didn't have any popcorn to munch on.

INTERMISSION

NOV. 12TH

A "COURTESY" TO MY READERS ...

Guys ... I probably shouldn't be sharing this with you, but ... I'm just too excited and I have to tell someone! Today at the Old Nick, well ... it seems that sometimes dreams really do come true.

There I was, performing my archivist duties (I still have some qualms there, but whatever) when I stumbled upon a treasure that has been lost to the world for many, MANY years. What was this forgotten gem you ask? Let's just say, for the sake of argument, that it concerned the blind daughter of a wealthy southern family, who despite her obvious handicap has a better grasp on the lives of her family than they do themselves. This, of course, leads to both laughter and tears, and the heroine, after several heart-breaking setbacks, ultimately finds love with a handsome and rich friend of the family. Roll credits.

Corny? Maybe by today's cynical standards. But some of us can still get swept up in a simple, elegant story told by people who were more concerned with advancing a magical new art form than making a quick buck. Sadly, they don't make them like this sweet, timeless tale anymore.

Not that I would have first-hand knowledge of the forgotten film in question. ;)

Sorry to be so cagey, but those of you who love old film as much as I do have by now figured out what I'm talking about. I wish I could tell you that soon you'll have a chance to experience what I experienced today, but alas, I do not currently wield that kind of influence in my chosen profession. But a girl can dream, right?

Anyway, hope I haven't teased too much. I hope to have an equally exciting day tomorrow, so I'm off to bed … if I can get to sleep. I'll see you lovelies on the silver screen! XOXO

CHAPTER THREE

The next morning, as she passed the lobby fountain, Muriel experienced a dim echo of the dream she'd had the night before. It had been a rough-reworking of *Blind Courtesy*, with Muriel naturally cast in the Delia Whitmore role, but instead of suffering from blindness like the film's heroine, Muriel could only see the world in the rich black-and-white hues of early cinema. The events that transpired were more drawn from her subconscious than from the movie itself, and Muriel had trouble recalling any real details, but she did remember something that happened in the dream's finale. She was rushing through a train station to tell a faceless man not to go, that she loved him but just hadn't been able to find the words, when something swept down at her from out of the sky. Whatever it was it had great wings and long black talons, and before she could scream, the horrible thing was shrieking and tearing at her face, waking her with a jolt.

This final, unpleasant detail had been buried until the sight of the winged figures on the fountain dredged it back up. Sadness crept in as she slumped up the stairs to the booth — a feeling that her dreaming mind, and her angels, had betrayed her.

She considered starting with the newer boxes, the ones that held prints of well-known and well-preserved titles, but she couldn't resist the temptation to scour the foul-smelling box for more lost gems. And to her delight, her temptation was immediately rewarded. The third tin she opened held an infamous, pre-code gangster picture titled *Knuckles Mahoney*, and if Muriel had her film history correct (and she was certain that she did), it had not seen the light of a projector since 1938. All of the reels were pristine and accounted for, making assemblage easy, and before she knew it, the print was threaded up and ready to roll.

But there was one thing missing. She simply could not endure another showing without some popcorn, so she rushed out to the corner convenience store to see what they had. Settling for a bag of the pre-popped kind, she bought the snack and hurried back to the theater, eager to get her matinee underway. When she arrived at the doors, a homeless woman was parked in front, a junk-filled shopping cart blocking the entrance. Muriel stood patiently waiting for the woman to move, to get on with her daily routine, but the woman just stared at the theater, at the boarded-up ticket booth, pulling some memory out of her addled, soggy brain.

Muriel cleared her throat, attempting to facilitate some sort of action, and the old crone turned to her, scowling with a pair of eyes that seemed clouded by smoke.

"I saw a picture there once," the woman said. "When I was a little girl. A horror picture. Dreadful film. Kept me up at night for weeks."

Muriel had deep sympathy for the homeless, especially the elderly, but the clock was ticking and she was anxious to get to her movie. "That's nice," Muriel said condescendingly. "I'm sorry, but I have to get inside."

"Nice?" The woman bristled. "Nothing nice about it! It was a dreadful film, just dreadful. Some kind of monster … with wings." The deep creases in her forehead became somehow more pronounced as she rifled through a long-troubled mind for more details. "A harpy! Yes, that's what it was … a harpy, like in Greek myth." Another pause. "Dreadful film."

There had to be something Muriel could do to move the woman along. The obvious finally dawned on her and she reached into her pack for a single crumpled bill. No sooner had she offered it when the dollar was snatched greedily from her hand. The poor old crone was not above charity, it would seem.

"You promise me one thing," she croaked. "If you find that movie in there, you burn it. Burn it to cinder!"

Though she had no intention of ever doing such a thing, Muriel wanted to get the crazy derelict out of her way, so she offered a placating nod. "I will. You have a nice day."

With a scoff, the crone pushed her cart on, rusty wheels squeaking her disapproval of the younger woman's patronizing. Muriel was too preoccupied to give it much thought, though, and five minutes later she was seated, center aisle as usual, happily crunching away as Knuckles Mahoney began what was certain to be a thrilling life of cinematic crime.

The film was pretty standard fare for the genre, and the actor who played Knuckles, a long-forgotten contract player named Miles Hoover, had nothing on the great screen gangsters portrayed by Jimmy Cagney or Edward G. Robinson. The production was chintzy for a 1930s studio picture, and Muriel found the story offensively misogynistic, even by the lax standards of the day. She was mentally composing a scathing review when the effects of the heavily greased, factory-packaged popcorn took hold, causing her to doze off.

As often happens to those who fall asleep during movies, Muriel's dreams fused with the narrative playing out onscreen, and in a devilish twist of irony, her subconscious cast her in the role of Cherry, one of Knuckles' poorly treated molls. Even stranger was that Muriel thrilled at being the gangster's play thing; every cruel word, infidelity, and slap was endured with a rush of dark, forbidden pleasure. When the vicious thug finally saw fit to ravage her, Muriel lost herself entirely, clawing at his pin-striped suit with garish nails, her moans of pleasure rising to a lurid pitch that would never make it past the MPAA censors. Her cries transitioned to the wail of sirens, and she and Knuckles were now on the run, hiding out in some old abandoned warehouse. The gangster promised that the cops would never take them alive, and when they burst through the doors, Tommy guns blazing, Muriel closed her eyes and prepared to die in a hail of bullets.

Instead, there was silence. She opened her eyes, finding the dream warehouse vast and empty, no sign of the cops or Knuckles Mahoney anywhere. She looked to the rafters and saw something perched there, hunched in a cluster of gray, filthy feathers. She thought that it must be some sort of strange barn owl, but when it spread its massive wings, wings too big for even a condor, that notion was dismissed. The creature swooped down, descending on her in a frenzy of flapping, and Muriel screamed as hand-sized talons tore at her face.

She awoke to find that the scream was not emitting from her own throat; it was blaring from the auditorium's archaic and rickety speaker system. The image onscreen was a mad flurry of frames, and Muriel's awakening brain figured something was going on with the projector — likely the print's two-strip audio track had gotten stuck in the gate and was causing the whole thing to jam up. In a daze she stumbled from her seat, adding bad popcorn to the already filthy floor, and raced out of the theater as fast as her feet would allow.

The scene in the booth was even worse than anticipated. The final reel was gummed so badly in the projector that it was shredding and peeling back on itself, like a banana being forced through a pinhole. Why the film didn't melt was anyone's guess, but Muriel, not waiting to find out, slammed down the power switch on the side of the lead projector. The machine rattled to a stop, and she did the same to projector two, nearly falling into panic as it violently hitched and seized. But then the monstrous old workhorse powered down with a sigh, and Muriel allowed herself to do the same. After a long, slow minute, her breathing caught up with her heart.

She had managed to save the machines, themselves valuable as museum pieces, but the print was another matter entirely. The distressed filmstrip had popped right off of the reel and was dangling out of the projector on to the unswept floor in a tangled lump. What remained in the projector was giving off an acrid, chemical stench, and it didn't take an expert to see that it was a total disaster. This was a murder scene, a restoration homicide, and Muriel was the prime and only suspect. The right thing to do would be to gather the salvageable materials, come clean with the matter, and accept the consequences with whatever dignity she could find.

But there was another option. If this was indeed a metaphorical murder, could she not consider the possibility of covering it up? No one knew what she had found here and therefore none would be the wiser if she just made it all go away. Did the world really need a restored print of *Knuckles Mahoney*? In truth, where was the crime in destroying a film that an enlightened film scholar such as herself had deemed dangerously regressive in its attitudes toward women? Wouldn't it be preferable to society on the whole that the cheap, nasty, little B-picture remain forgotten, that chauvinists and rapists not to be given more fuel for their sick fantasies, that they be denied a new icon to emulate like the mobster hero of *Scarface* or the serial murderers of *Natural Born Killers*? And if keeping this heroic act a secret meant that Muriel was able to keep her job ... would that be such a terrible thing?

Yes, she decided. This was the right thing to do. So without further deliberation, she gathered the mangled reel off the floor and stuffed it into her backpack. She considered allowing the undamaged reels to remain behind; it wouldn't be hard to claim that the print was found with a reel missing. But the more she thought about it, the more she wanted the whole film gone. So she emptied her backpack of all other items and fit the rest of the print inside. Then she bolted out the door, a criminal fleeing the scene of the crime.

She was past the fountain and almost out the front doors when she ran into, almost quite literally, Kurt and Kitt.

"Muriel!" Kurt greeted as the fleeing girl skidded to a halt right in front of him. "We just came by to check up on your progress."

"Uh, yeah, well," Muriel stammered. "Not much to report I'm afraid." She shifted the overstuffed pack on her shoulder, attempting to shield it from their prying eyes.

Kurt and Kitt shared a mild look of bewilderment. "Really?" Kurt questioned. "There was a whole stack of film boxes in the projection booth last time we checked."

"Well, I haven't gone through all of it yet. But so far all I've found are titles that are readily available." She tried to maintain a chirpy tone, despite feeling as though she was being, albeit deservedly, interrogated. "But hope springs eternal!"

With their eerily similar eyes, Kurt and Kitt shared a look of skepticism, then re-directed at Muriel, smiling in unison. "If you don't mind," Kurt said. "I think we'll have a look."

Muriel's stomach dropped. Up there in the booth, sitting on her editing table were five reels of *Blind Courtesy*, clearly discovered and tampered with. Once her bosses saw that they would know she was lying, and when they looked in her bag, they'd find what remained of *Knuckles Mahoney* and assume she intended to steal it. Then, in addition to losing her job, she would likely be brought up on criminal charges. The jig, as Knuckles might say, was up.

She was about to crack, to confess to it all, when something chimed inside Kitt's designer purse. The wire-framed blonde scrunched her perfect Aryan nose and pulled out her smartphone, answering the call. "Yes?" she barked into the device. "Christ, Phil, are you sure?" A weary sigh followed. "Fine, we'll be right there."

"What was it?" Kurt asked with concern.

"There was a mix-up at the Egyptian. The new print of *Playtime* is missing a reel."

And like that, a bullet was dodged. Kurt and Kitt rushed off to deal with the crisis at the Egyptian, leaving Muriel in the lobby, flushed with adrenaline and relief. Somewhere, someone had been watching out for her, and glancing back at the fountain, she couldn't help but feel that it must have been her angels. She offered them a solemn, sincere appreciation and promised that she would never, ever do anything like this again. A few blocks from her house she ditched the pack in a lonely dumpster, and that was the last anyone would know of *Knuckles Mahoney.*

CHAPTER FOUR

After a restless, guilt-fueled sleep, Muriel returned to the Old Nick the following morning and was relieved to find that Kurt and Kitt had not been back to inspect the prints in the booth. The circular tins that housed the now discarded print sat there, empty accusers, reminding Muriel that she would have to dispose of them as well if she hoped to keep her crime a secret. But without her backpack, there was no way to sneak them out, and she couldn't risk just walking out the door with them, especially in light of her employer's unannounced visit the day before. An idea struck her, and she went back to the boxes, searching for a print that had been packed without a tin. To her surprise, at the bottom of the rattiest box, she found one.

Collecting it the best she could, she brought the print over to the table to see what sort of movie deserved to be treated this shabbily. Shockingly, the film was remarkably well preserved, a miracle considering it had been left unprotected for so many years. It was the right number of reels to substitute for *Knuckles Mahoney*, so it would seem that Muriel's promise to the angels had been heard and accepted. All she had to do was pack the mystery print into the tins and no one would ever be the wiser. She would even leave it for Kurt and Kitt to discover, let them have the glory all to themselves. It was the punishment Muriel rightly deserved.

Resolved, she reached for the film, and the end spilled from the table like a snake fleeing the grip of its handler. As she bent over to retrieve the dangling strip, she caught a glimpse of the images repeated in the frames, advancing incrementally like pictures in a flip book. Images that haunted some part of her subconscious, demanding they be given a closer look.

Don't do it, Muriel told herself. *Just wrap this thing as tight as you can, cram it in to those tins, and don't forget to tear off the labels. Do not push your luck any further.*

Though it killed her to do so, Muriel was able to stick to her guns and pack up the film without giving it another look. But she decided not to tell her superiors about the find until she had a night to sleep on it, so she busied herself with tidying work and went home later that day with the haunting images still spooling behind her retinas. It wasn't until she was home, sitting in front of her laptop, that she recalled the strange interaction with the homeless woman outside the theater the day before. A few keystrokes later and she was drawn into the mystery, like a hound chasing a rabbit down a deep and fascinating hole.

INTERMISSION

NOV. 14th

NOT TO "HARP" ON ABOUT IT, BUT…

As most of you know, I am not the biggest horror fan, but recently I have taken a … let's call it an *interest* in an obscure film from the 30s that reportedly scared the bejesus out of folks back in the day. The movie in question is *Shriek of the Harpy* and it was released by a fly-by-night production house named Anvil Pictures in a shameless attempt to capitalize on the Universal Monsters craze. The German auteur director, Rudolph Meiner, was so embittered by the course of his Hollywood career that he returned home to the Fatherland and joined up with the Nazi party after Hitler invaded Poland. Though Meiner was never heard of again after the war, some accounts place him at a concentration camp that was stormed by the allies, and it is presumed that he was shot and killed in the battle. Good riddance, I say!

As for *Shriek of the Harpy*, the general consensus seems to be that it was a reasonably effective chiller with a standard script and some notable directorial flourishes from Meiner, who was a protégé, at least in spirit, to F.W. Murnau. The titular Harpy was inspired by the monsters of Greek myth, and the creature design by legendary make-up artist Charlie Spears was said to have been quite shocking by the standards of the time. But the thing that was remembered most by the small number of people who saw *Shriek of the Harpy* was the blood-curdling sound the Harpy made when it attacked its victims, the "shriek", as it were. It was a sound so awful that it gave viewers nightmares for weeks afterward, a claim that at least one viewer I have personally spoken to can support. Sound designers were not credited in films of that era, so we may never know who was responsible for the remarkable noise, but whoever they were, by all accounts they did their job maybe a little too well.

While all of this is fascinating, the thing about *Shriek of the Harpy* that interests me is the well-documented rumors that it was horribly, horribly misogynistic. I mean, hello, the movie is about a monster woman who is literally a harpy! Not too subtle there, Gustav! And Meiner is certainly the one to blame — while the screenplay was credited to writer Eugene Torrance, the story is a creation of Meiner's fevered brain and Torrance later even apologized for scripting it, calling the finished film, "Sick, chauvinistic dreck." (Sad footnote: Torrance hung himself at the age of 40 in the barn of his country home. His body was found swinging from the rafters, watched over by a pair of hooting barn owls.) Needless to say, my interest is piqued.

Lordy, have I rambled tonight! Well, off to bed sweeties. If anyone has any more info pertaining to this lost "treasure," please let me know. I have a teeny weeny hunch that we have not heard the last of the Harpy's terrifying shriek. ☺

CHAPTER FIVE

Powerless against her curiosity, Muriel raced to the theater the following morning, yanked the changeling print out of the *Knuckles Mahoney* tins, and slapped it down on her editing table to have another look. Sure enough, staring back at her in a lurid, dripping font was the title "Shriek of the Harpy". In this, her third major discovery, Muriel had stumbled upon a Holy Grail film for horror fans. Except that no one would ever know she was the one to discover it. Of course, she could take credit and boast about it online, but her claims on the internet would not be taken seriously by the fans who posted in the forums. And in terms of seeing it — well, she would have to wait with all the other chumps, if they day ever came when some distributor released it.

Across the room, the projectors called to her. Muriel fell into a fevered trance, and an hour later she was standing before the twin iron hulks, now fully loaded and ready to roll on the film. A force had possessed her, a facet of her barely cognizant mind that *demanded* she bear witness to this cinematic atrocity. What was needed, she rationalized, was to face the film's transgressions head-on, to be incensed and offended by its backwards misogyny so that she might arrive at a keen and thoughtful dissertation, casting a healing light into a dark corner of cinema history. Yes, it was crucial — *important* — that Muriel Sharpe view this terrible film, and nothing but a private, immediate screening would suffice.

She stood there, finger trembling over the lead projector's power switch. Here was the moment of truth. She could back out now, leave *Shriek of the Harpy* to Kurt and Kitt and be done with all of this madness. She could do as she was told, follow orders, and be the good girl. The nice, subservient girl who allowed her male superior to swoop in and claim all of the credit she so richly deserved.

She threw the switch, ran down into the theater, and was in her preferred seat right as the melting candle wax title appeared on the screen.

The plot unfolded in a manner quite typical of a 1930s horror picture. It concerned a young couple, Adelaide and Calvin, who travel from an unspecified city to visit a friend who has taken up residence in a country manor inherited from his wealthy, recently deceased parents. Once there, the cheerful couple find that their friend, Rupert, is mercilessly henpecked by his shrew (one might even describe her as a harpy) of a wife, Nellie Rae. The constant nagging of his gold-digging spouse drives Rupert into the only place on the estate where he can find solace — the aviary, a magnificent bird sanctuary built by his dead father.

When the brilliantly realized aviary set appeared onscreen, Muriel's heart palpitated. It wasn't the room itself that caused the reaction; though cleverly designed as a dome-like cage, there was nothing unsettling about it save for the fluttering and chirping of the live, on-set birds. The feature that spooked Muriel was the room's centerpiece — an ornate fountain adorned with grim, winged statuary. It was an uncanny cousin to the fountain that sat crumbling in the lobby; so much so that Muriel reasoned that they both must have been carved by the same sculptor. A slow panic gripped her as she tried to reconcile the coincidence, reasoning that the designers of the Old Nick had somehow taken this film as the inspiration for the lobby's focal point. But in her heart, Muriel knew that the idea was patently absurd.

In the aviary, Rupert discovers a parchment hidden by his father that appears to detail some sort of occult spell. Adelaide intrudes, attempting to coax Rupert out of his shell, but the gesture backfires when the married man professes his undying love for her. Flustered by the advance, Adelaide flees, not realizing that Nellie Rae has been eavesdropping the whole time. Using her husband's failed indiscretion as leverage, Nellie threatens Rupert with a costly and humiliating divorce, and their heated arguing drives the birds into a state of agitated cheeping. The sound causes Rupert to explode, to toss off the shackles of civility by grabbing Nellie and shaking her violently. She responds by clawing him across the face, and in murderous retaliation, he pushes her into the fountain's pool and forces her head under the water. The birds take to the air, swarming in a furious cloud of feathers as Nellie struggles in Rupert's death-grip, drowning to the flapping of their wings.

Though the scene was staged to downplay the violence of the murder, Muriel still found it wholly distasteful. The character of Nellie Rae was written to be so loathsome that the viewer sympathized with Rupert's decision to kill her, and her shrill portrayal by an unappealing and rightly forgotten contract player didn't help matters. But the real blame lay in Meiner's cruel direction — his distaste for women was palpable beyond the words that sprung from the actors' mouths. *What strong-handed matron had beaten this attitude into him?* Muriel wondered. *What emasculating trauma had informed his viewpoint, warped his personality into something so vile that it demanded to be poured into every scene, every shot, every hateful frame?* Since the dawn of cinema, female leads had suffered under the attack of monsters, but there was a sadistic quality ingrained in *Shriek of the Harpy* that went beyond simply placing damsels in distress. You could sense Meiner behind the camera, leering as his violent fantasies were trapped in celluloid, and easily imagine the pleasure he would take in the back of a darkened theater, watching women squirm in their seats while the men sat smirking next to them.

Shockingly, Meiner allowed the character of Rupert to feel remorse, but it soon became apparent where all of this was leading. Using his father's witchcraft, Rupert attempts to raise his wife from her watery tomb, his efforts nothing but an act of madness witnessed by the birds. In a moment of restored sanity, Rupert tears up the parchment and throws it into the pool, and that's when things take a turn for the supernatural. The birds settle back on their perches, like churchgoers seating themselves at mass, and as they watch silently, some-thing rises from the pool of the fountain. But it is not Nellie — at least not anymore. Great wings crest, shaking off water, and gnarled claws grasp at the fountain's lip, lifting up a terrifying figure. Emerg-ing in Nellie's stead is the Harpy, a distinctly female monster spoken of fearfully in myth, said to occupy a strata of Hell reserved for suicides and those who profit from murder. A head flared with feathers lowers its piercing gaze at the stunned and terrified Rupert, and out of its beak bursts a terrible, soul-wrenching shriek.

As had been reported, the sound was unforgettable and deafening. It shook the theater from floor to rafters and for a moment Muriel feared that the sagging old ceiling was about to cave in from the stress. Thankfully the scene cut away, taking the awful sound and the briefly glimpsed Harpy with it. But those eyes — silvery, piercing, and locked in a tight shot — stayed with Muriel long after the frame faded into the next scene. She told herself that they were a trick of makeup, primitive contact lenses, but she could not shake them out of her mind. The scared little girl that still lived in her heart believed that those eyes — and the monster they belonged to — were real.

The next few reels passed like a nightmare as the Harpy unleashes its terror upon the household. Rupert avoids death by fleeing into the night, but a pretty, young housemaid who comes to clean the aviary is not so fortunate. The death toll increases with every following scene as one hapless servant after another meets their grisly fate at the talons of the Harpy. Keeping with the censoring parameters of the time, the deaths were not graphically depicted, but Muriel found them to be far more visceral and suggestive than similar scenes in either the Universal or Val Lewton horror canon. The lurid method in which Meiner utilized his camera — a subtle hint of motion here or a lingering of a shot there — suggested that the deaths were violent, protracted, and painful. It was a total affront to Muriel's sense of good taste, yet as the picture barreled towards its inevitable climax, she found it impossible to pry her eyes from the screen.

The prerequisite horror movie thunderstorm descends on the manor, and when Calvin and Adelaide discover the maid and butler dead, they attempt to leave, only to find that their car is stuck in the mud dredged up by the rainwater. Back inside they are greeted by the disheveled and raving Rupert — also driven back indoors by the storm — and naturally the young couple assumes that he must be the killer. But Rupert insists that the deaths are the work of the Harpy, a creature he has summoned from Hell, and when Calvin attempts to call the authorities to take the ranting lunatic into custody, he finds the phone lines have been taken down by the storm. A shadow falls upon the living room skylight, and Rupert cowers by the fireplace, screaming that the Harpy has come for him at last. Calvin and Adelaide are convinced that his mind is completely broken, but when the Harpy shatters through the skylight, Rupert's ravings are proven all too true.

Shown at last in its full glory, the creature design for the Harpy, though exceptional for the time, was no more convincing than the iconic but lovably hokey make-ups for the classic versions of Frankenstein, the Wolf Man, or the Mummy. The actress who played Nellie

Rae had been transformed into a monstrous angel of death with great black wings and a crown of feathers that crested from her head into twin horns. The woman's fine narrow nose had been re-sculpted into a beak, and those piercing, silvery eyes were framed by thick rings of dark mascara. She wore a Greek tunic-style dress that barely covered her ample breasts, and when she raised her hands, they were re-figured into four-fingered, birdlike talons. By today's standards, the monster design was quaint and would likely elicit laughter from a jaded, special effects-savvy crowd, but Muriel's suspension of disbelief was strong and well-fortified, and to her, the Harpy was as terrifying now as the moment it landed on set.

The Harpy lunged for the camera and Muriel jolted back, as if it was going to fly off the screen and attack her. Calvin stepped in to defend Adelaide, attempting to ward the monster off with a fireplace poker, but the Harpy swatted the weapon away like an insult. The creature attacked poor Calvin with both talons, raking long swaths of blood down his blandly handsome face. This sort of grisly violence was unheard of in films of this era, and even though the black and white muted what full color would have made plain, the effect was shocking just the same. Adelaide screamed and Muriel looked away, not able to face whatever horror came next. The Harpy shrieked, rumbling the theater, and Muriel was shaken to the core, certain that the sound was coming from somewhere other than the auditorium speakers. There was a great crashing noise from something outside, and suddenly everything went black.

Muriel sat there in stunned silence, thinking for a terrible moment that the world had come to an end. Then there was another teeth-chattering rumble, and she recognized it as the sound of thunder — and not the canned sound effect you heard time and time again in old movies. There was a storm outside, just like in the movie, but this storm was real and was likely the cause of the power outage. Muriel felt a rush of relief, but that gratitude faded quickly to annoyance at the inconvenience of her show being disrupted.

"Godammit," she cursed. The room was ink black, the row of seats barely visible in front of her, and rummaging through her pockets she realized that her phone with its helpful onboard flashlight was sitting on the editing table upstairs. Turning to the back of the theater, she stood and began to fumble her way around, hoping she could find her way back to the booth without injury. After that, she could try for the breaker room, but she highly doubted that this blackout was a simple blown fuse. The power was likely out for the entire city block, and she would be lucky if she could repack the print and get out of here using only the light of her phone.

She was almost under the balcony when the thunder crashed again, freezing her dead in her tracks. When the scare passed, she laughed out loud, feeling foolish for allowing herself to get so spooked. "Silly girl," she scolded herself playfully.

A shattering, shrill sound atomized the air around her, and Muriel's soul practically jumped out of her skin. It was the shriek of the Harpy, but his time it was not diffused through the safety glass of cinema fantasy — this time it was real and in the room with her. Muriel looked about, wide-eyed, searching for falling plaster, broken glass, twisted metal, something, anything that would rationally explain the noise, but all she could see was the darkness closing in on her, and all she could sense was the certainty that she wasn't alone.

The shriek came again, louder and closer this time. Glancing upwards, she could see it now, a great shadowy shape perched on the lip of the balcony, silver eyes gleaming in the dark. The Harpy had come for her, demanding that she answer for her crimes, and despite knowing the fullness of terror, Muriel couldn't help but be awed by the spread of its magnificent wings.

The monster swooped from the balcony and Muriel dove into the nearest row, landing hard on the cement with her knees. She yelped as air rushed past her head, blowing her hair back in the gust of a rustling wings. The shriek blasted again furiously, and a steady flapping indicated that the Harpy was circling for another dive. Stooped in a painful crouch, Muriel scuttled down the row, careful to keep her head lower than the seats. She was almost out into the aisle when talons tore at her back.

Muriel screamed and thrashed her arms around as if attacked by an angry swarm of bees, but after a few seconds it became apparent that she was swatting at empty air. Breathing heavy, she scanned quickly around, and touching her shoulder she found no wounds, just the unmarred fabric of her T-shirt. The Harpy, if still in the auditorium, had gone silently to ground, leaving Muriel standing alone with just the seats and the white vastness of the movie screen. If the Harpy had ever been there at all, that is.

Tears began to well up in her eyes, but instead of crying, she broke into hysterical laughter. Madness. This was all madness. There was no flying monster loose in the theater. The stress of the job, the guilt over trashing a print, the crushing loneliness and self-doubt with which she was in constant denial — one or a combination of these things had pushed Muriel Sharpe over the edge. The right thing to do would be to call her parents and tell them that she had cracked up, suffered some sort of nervous breakdown. Lord knows it wouldn't come as a surprise. Yes, that's what she would do — she would walk calmly out of this theater, go get some help, and leave the world of film preservation, and this godforsaken place, behind.

Feeling the fool, Muriel limped out of the auditorium, stumbling into the lobby to the startling crash of more thunder and the disorienting strobe of lightning flashes. The rain was coming down so hard that the domed ceiling had sprung fist-sized leaks, showering water into the fountain's pool, filling it to a frothing brim. From their perches, Muriel's beloved cherubs glared down, their once kindly faces full of scorn, their cheeks streaming with bitter, rain-water tears. There was no comfort to be taken from them anymore; now they were harbingers of doom.

As she neared the fountain, Muriel slipped on a wet tile and was driven down to her already agonized knees. She cursed and spat and blamed the cherubs, reaching for the lip of the large pool to haul herself up. Before her fingers could find purchase, however, a hand that was not hers slapped down on the lip. A clawed, four-fingered talon.

"Oh God," Muriel stammered as the Harpy rose from the fountain's pool, exactly as it had in the movie. Lightning flashed again, illuminating the creature, and Muriel could see that unlike its cinematic counterpart, this Harpy was realistic and entirely convincing. Greasy black feathers sprouted from mottled gray flesh, and its beak, no mere make-up job, was tapered into a razor-keen point. It extended its wings to their full glory, shaking off water in an icy spray, spattering Muriel's terrified face. The eyes — those terrible eyes — narrowed as it opened its beak, and when it shrieked, a slimy tongue probed forth like a worm seeking decay.

Muriel didn't even realize that she had gotten to her feet until she stumbled back and crashed through the auditorium doors. Her mind was waging a war between shock and hysteria with sanity caught in the crossfire, still hoping that this was all some vividly realized nightmare. Thankfully, adrenaline flooded to the rescue, clearing the fog of terror, allowing her to snap into crisis mode. She scanned the area for something — *anything* — that could be used as a defense, and her eyes fell upon a velvet stanchion rope that had rolled under the seats five decades past. Picking it up, she ran for the doors, reaching them just as the flapping, screeching horror was closing the distance. She pulled the doors shut and wrapped the thick, moldy rope through the brass handles, tying it off into a makeshift barricade. The Harpy slammed into the other side, shrieking in vengeful protest.

The obstruction was not going to hold the monster at bay for long, so Muriel quickly set about finding an escape route. She ran to the front of the theater, to the exits on either side of the screen, but both had been bricked up to keep out vandals and squatters. The only clear way out was back through the auditorium doors and past the Harpy, an option Muriel was not about to consider.

There was the possibility of trying to escape through the balcony, but she couldn't remember if the upstairs exits were boarded up or not. The question was moot anyway, as there was no way to access the balcony from the auditorium, not unless she could convince the Harpy to give her a lift. Whatever amusement Muriel took from that thought was obliterated by the splintering of the barricaded doors, and she furiously looked for someplace to hide. They only place that could even warrant consideration was the crawlspace that separated the movie screen from the theater wall, a space that measured no more than a foot across. Cursing her inability to commit to a diet, Muriel squeezed into the crawlspace and hoped for the best.

She fit, but just barely. The last of her body was pulled into the space when she heard the auditorium doors smash open with a mad flurry of wings.

The Harpy made guttural chirping noises as it swooped around the auditorium, seeking out its prey. It was only a matter of time before it sussed out where Muriel had hidden, so if she intended to mount some form of defense, she had better do it fast. As if in answer to her prayers, her eyes caught the dull gleam of metal lying on the crawlspace floor, not more than three feet away. Looking closer, she recognized it as the head of a hammer, and as the hideous, unnatural being flapped and chattered just beyond the barrier of the screen, Muriel squeezed further into the crawlspace to reach the weapon-ready tool.

With incredible effort, she strained, reaching down and hooking a finger under the cloven head. She lifted her hand, balancing the hammer from her fingertips until it was close enough for her other hand to grab it by the handle. Her awkward positioning, though, caused her hand to jostle, and the hammer fell loose and clattered back to the floor.

The sound of feet landing was heard from the other side of the screen, and a winged silhouette stood there, listening. Muriel held every muscle in her body still, hoping that the creature would be thrown off by her silence and lack of movement. In her terror, Muriel tried to reason what sort of mind — animal, human, or otherwise — the Harpy possessed. Did it think? Could it be bargained with? It did possess feminine attributes. Was there a possibility, however small, that she could appeal to it on that level, one woman to another?

"Hello?" Muriel asked the silhouette. "Can we talk?"

Silence. Not so much as a chirp. "Look … You don't have to do this. Just let me go and you'll never see me again. We can keep this between us girls. I won't even tell anyone I ever saw you. Girl Scout's honor."

The silhouette cocked its flared head, and for a moment Muriel actually believed that the creature had heard her. *I did it!* she convinced herself. *I got through to it. To her.*

But then the Harpy gave its answer, an inhuman shriek, letting it be known once and for all that there was no soft, feminine side to be reached. It lunged forth with murderous intent, talons raking at the screen, tearing away strips in long, jagged rivers. In a final desperate move, Muriel reached again for the hammer, managing to grasp the handle in her cramped and sweaty palm. There was a loud ripping sound as the Harpy tore into the crawlspace, and Muriel swung upwards with all her strength, striking the monster hard on the beak.

The Harpy stumbled back, talons clawing at the air. *How you like me now, bitch?* was Muriel's silent retort. The creature shook off the pain with a rustle of feathers, and Muriel swung again, this time hitting it on the scowling crest of its head. The fiend screamed and spat and took to the air, and Muriel ran for the auditorium exit, which had been left wide open in the Harpy's destructive wake.

Muriel charged into the lobby and, forgetting about the slick tile, went sliding across the floor, smashing her body into the basin of the fountain's pool. The Old Nick's ceiling was now a giant colander, showering down rainwater and soaking Muriel to her already shivering bones. As she pulled herself up to make a final dash for the doors, the Harpy flew in from the auditorium, screeching in hateful triumph. It landed in a crouch right in front of the doors, and when it rose to its full height, the spread of its wings blotted out all routes — and all hope — of escape.

To the right were the marble stairs that led to the projection booth, and without fully understanding what she was doing, Muriel ran for them. She took the slippery stairs two steps at a time, expecting the Harpy to descend on her at any moment and tear her to shreds. The monster never came at her, however, and she reached the booth winded and shaking but otherwise intact. She slammed the door shut, then grabbed an old chair to wedge under the doorknob, knowing full well that it wouldn't hold the creature back for long. It gave her a moment to catch her breath, though, and allowed her frantic mind to formulate some sort of plan.

The room was dark, but after some fumbling she was able to locate her bag and, in a nice bit of luck, came upon a penlight, which meant she wouldn't have to use up what little was left of her phone's battery. She dug her cell out of the bottom and was about to call 9-1-1 when she realized how insane her story was going to sound. Instead, she called Kurt and, getting his voicemail, left a message that there was an emergency and he needed to come to the theater right away. As soon as she hung up, the battery died.

She turned her light to the projectors where *Shriek of the Harpy* sat threaded, waiting to play out its grand finale. It dawned on Muriel that perhaps, as crazy as it all sounded, the manner in which the Harpy was destroyed in the film would be the key to destroying it here in the real world. Old horror movies always had happy endings, and unlike the slasher films of the 80s, when the monsters died in the classics they stayed dead, at least until the cheaply made sequel. And *Shriek of the Harpy* had earned no sequel.

Muriel ran to the projector, tore out the final reel, and dragged the last few feet of film over to her editing table, not even bothering to detach the print from the machine. Grabbing the looking glass, she held the penlight in her teeth and furiously scrolled through the final reel, doing her damnedest to suss out the plot.

The climax predictably took place in the aviary with the three principles and the Harpy present. There were shots that seemed to indicate Adelaide was attempting to reason with the monster (as Muriel had done), but ultimately it turns on the true guilty party, Rupert. Muriel hurried through the frames of Rupert being mauled by the vengeful creature, but the killing seemed to go on and on for several feet of film. Finally, the scene cut to Calvin recovering the parchment, and in a desperate move, he throws it into the fountain, which calls up some sort dimensional vortex from the depths. The Harpy follows the parchment into the vortex, and as lightning strikes the manor and sets it aflame, the young heroes escape. The last shot was of the couple standing arm in arm, watching the manor burn to the ground as the final title card announced that in no uncertain terms this was "THE END".

So that was it. She had to destroy the parchment — throw it into the fountain, which would then create a dimensional vortex that would summon the Harpy back to Hell. Only there was no parchment. There was no magical document of any kind. All Muriel had was the fountain in the lobby …

… and the film itself. Perhaps the print of *Shriek of the Harpy* was the parchment, the magical MacGuffin around which this entire nightmare revolved. Yes, that had to be it! It was the only thing in this insane situation that made any kind of sense.

Something crashed through the projection window and a tornado of dust and feathers exploded into the room. Muriel instinctively grabbed her scissors from the table as the Harpy picked itself up off the floor, once again rising to its full terrifying height. Its wings were folded around its body like a protective cloak, but when Muriel flinched at it, wielding the scissors like a dagger, the wings spread to their furthest breadth. Then it shrieked at her with such force that her eardrums erupted into spasms.

Acting on blind instinct, Muriel lunged with the scissors, stabbing them right above the monster's ample, womanly breasts. The creature's silvery eyes widened into glistening pools of shock and it withdrew, clawing at the handle of the scissors, attempting to pull them out. Muriel wasn't going to wait to see if it succeeded. She scooped up what she could of the print and fled the room, trailing film in her panicked wake.

Out in the lobby, the storm had built to a crescendo, the crashing sound of thunder nearly drowned by a thousand tiny waterfalls pouring through the ceiling. Muriel stumbled down the stairs until a dangling loop of film tripped her up and sent her sprawling the rest of the way. But there wasn't any time for pain. She struggled to her feet, wrapped the tangle of film around her in a death shroud, and launched herself towards the fountain.

But *Shriek of the Harpy* did not want to let her go. It tightened around her like a constricting snake; sharp, sprocket-holed edges sliced into her, death by a million paper cuts. It tripped her up again at the fountain, causing her to smash into it with her shins, sending white flashes through her body like electric jolts. Screaming in both pain and frustration, she ripped and tore at the print until her hands were bloody, but the celluloid was seemingly forged of steel.

Finally, she gathered a handful and shoved it into the pool like a homicidal mother drowning an unwanted child. Then she waited for the portal to appear.

At first, nothing happened — no change in the surface of the water — and Muriel nearly burst into tears. But then there were ripples, and then a churning, and soon a small whirlpool had formed, opening a fissure into some terrible world beyond. Despite the nightmarish implications of such a world, Muriel was so happy to see it, so happy that it was real, that she broke into hysterical gales of laughter.

A shriek of torment carried over Muriel's cackling and she froze, staring blankly into the rushing vortex of the pool. The air came alive behind her, charged with the flapping of great wings, and Muriel knew that the Harpy was diving in to attack. She could not bear to face that horrible thing again, could not stomach the thought of those terrible eyes being the last thing she saw, so she tensed and waited for the talons to rip her apart like human taffy. But there came no pain, only a splash and a spray of water, and Muriel opened her eyes to see the Harpy torpedoing into the vortex after the rapidly sinking print. Then both the monster and the film from which it was spawned were gone.

"Muriel?" a voice asked behind her. Muriel whipped around to find Kurt standing there, flustered and confused. "What in heaven's name is going on around here?"

That was a really good question. Muriel would have loved to explain it, to tell him the story of how she had saved herself and defeated a monster by drowning a rare film print in a fountain pool, but all evidence of the nightmare — the vortex, the Harpy ... even the storm — were gone as if they had never happened. No one would ever believe her, and at this point, Muriel wasn't sure that she could believe it herself. All she could do was throw her head back and laugh.

And she kept on laughing for a very long time.

CLOSING CREDITS

NOV. 26th

I'M BACK!

SO … gentle reader, your favorite (former, maybe one day again … whatever) film archivist has returned with another update. Right now I'm blogging from my parents as I have been released into their custody for the Thanksgiving holiday. "Custody?" you ask? Yes, well, that's a story, isn't it? Suffice it to say, Muriel Sharpe has suffered a mild breakdown, at least that's the official version. I've spent the last few weeks in the beautiful and palatial Angel Memorial clinic where I've been treated for what the doctors are calling a "brief psychotic episode." Sounds crazy (pun intended), right? Yeah, well, what can I say? Girl's got an active imagination … I guess. Jury's still out on that one as far as I'm concerned. Regardless, I'm on some serious medication, and not the fun kind. My doctors (all male, of course … hello "female hysteria" diagnosis!) say I may need to be on it for the rest of my life. As if "my life" couldn't get any better!

(That last part was sarcasm BTW)

Since the cat (or bird more accurately) is now out of the bag, let's just say that my unauthorized movie screenings did not have a healthy effect on my pretty little brain. Somehow I got the idea that the monster from *Shriek of the Harpy* was attacking me and I ended up stabbing one of my bosses (Kitt, the fembot) in the shoulder with some scissors when she surprised me in the projection booth. (She's alive, thank the goddess, and not pressing charges as long as I stay in therapy). Then my other boss found me in the lobby, trying to drown the horror movie print in the creepy old fountain that some lunatic decided to build there. Yeah, quite a scene, I know. Needless to say, I lost my job, got sent to the booby hatch, and here we are, back at mom and dad's. What an awesome start to my career! Yay me!

(Again, sarcasm people, look it up)

So that pretty much brings us up to speed. But before I go … and not sure when I'll be back…it depends how I respond to "treatment" … I do want to issue a mild warning: That stupid, misogynistic (and Holy Hell is it misogynistic … but more on that someday) movie was rescued from my drowning attempt and has been fully restored. There is already a major home video release planned, and no, I won't be credited for finding it, thanks for asking. Now I won't claim that *Shriek of the Harpy* will have the same effect on you as it did on your intrepid blogger, but I do urge you NOT to give this EVIL film your time, attention, or money. For horror fans, I know that the temptation might prove too great, especially with the film's sordid reputation, but I'm begging you, PLEASE just let this hateful piece of celluloid fade back into obscurity where it belongs. If you hear the Harpy's shriek calling you, I'm begging, BEGGING you to ignore it.

Aaaaaaaaaaaand someone in a film forum I frequent just posted that the studio who owns the rights has already announced a remake. PERFECT.

GRAVE MARKER

Russell Coy

THE ONE
WHO LIES NEXT
TO YOU

Chapter 1

Angie felt a single, silent buzzing against her thigh. She groaned softly.

Great. Wonderful. Just what I goddamn need.

She started to pull her cell from her pocket. The door behind her creaked and clicked shut, and then a voice said, "Okay, Ange." She returned the phone to her pocket, could guess how the text would read anyway.

Carol Drake walked into her line of sight with a Styrofoam cup in one hand, a sheaf of papers in the other. She went behind her desk and set the items down, sat in her rolling black chair, and leaned forward.

"So," she said. "I've heard Marcia's side of the story. Now, I want you to tell me what happened. Your side of things."

Angie took a breath, kept her face blank but for the slight raising of an eyebrow. "My side is I did my job. I've told Marcia, repeatedly in the past, she can't leave empty skids out in the aisles. Yet, she keeps on doing it."

Carol nodded and rubbed one eye with her thumb. "Okay, well, we're not talking about what Marcia did right now, are we? What did you do?"

Angie shrugged. "I handled it."

"Handled it, how?"

"I went to the break room, got her, and brought her back to the warehouse. I showed her the skid and told her to put it away."

Carol looked down at the papers in front of her, moved her lips without noise. Then out loud, she said, "You mean, you walked into the break room and up to Marcia, told her to 'Get your ass up and come with me right now', and when she didn't move, you kicked over the chair beside her and said …" Carol flipped to the next page. "… 'You want me to drag you with me by the hair?'"

"I wouldn't say …"

"And then, when you reached the aisle and showed her the skid, instead of letting her use the pallet jack, you made her drag it with her bare hands over to the skid stack."

She leaned back and made a fish-tail motion with her hand. "Sound about right?"

Angie gave a defeated sigh. "Look, bring her in here and I'll apologize, okay? I'm just … I'm having a really bad day, and this is just one more thing I can't handle right now."

Carol let out a harsh breath and leaned her head back with her eyes closed. "Angie, you know it's not just you whose ass is on the line, right? I recommended you for this job. If you get a reputation for bullying team members, I don't look very good either."

"I wasn't bullying anyone."

"According to Marcia, you were. Do you know that she got a splinter while dragging that skid?"

"Oh, for Christ's sake," Angie hissed. "Look, you know just like I do that Marcia Cranmore's a lazy cunt who thinks she only has to do what she feels like and dump the rest on everyone else. Now, tell me where I'm in the wrong for doing something about it."

"Stop." Carol raised her eyebrows and pointed a finger at Angie. "You are way the hell out of line talking to me like that, and do not think I won't write you up."

"Well, take out your forms and write me the fuck up, then!" Angie unfolded her arms and leaned forward. "You know, I bust my ass for this place. I've been nothing but a hard worker from day one, so if you're going to take Marcia's side, of all people, then I might as well not give a shit anymore."

It was on that last sentence Angie heard her voice crack, and felt the hot mist in her eyes.

"Ange, are you okay?"

"Huh? Yeah." She wiped the corner of her eye as discreetly as she could. "Look, I'm, uh ... I'm sorry, Carol. Like I said, it's been a bad day."

"I can see that. Well, you know, it hasn't been peaches for me, either, exactly."

"I know. I'm ... Look, just do what you think is right. I know I was out of line. I've always hated when bosses take their shit out on people under them. I thought I was better than that." She shrugged. "Maybe I'm not."

For a moment, the only sound was the rapping of manicured nails on the desk.

"You know," Carol said, "if you were anyone else, I would have sent you home two minutes ago."

Angie stifled an unwanted giggle. "Well, that would be the perfect punishment, believe me."

A bitter smile settled on her face. She looked up. Carol was staring at her, but no longer with anger.

"Ange, is there something going on? Something you want to get off your chest?"

Chapter 2

The apple-cinnamon smell of a Glade Plug-In caught Angie's nose, and beneath it was a faraway scent of kitty litter. It was getting dull, just sitting on the couch, waiting. Angie leaned over, lifted a paperback from the coffee table, and read the back cover.

"Having fun, Snoopy?"

She jumped at Carol's sudden presence at the arm of the sofa.

"Sorry," she said, placing the book back on the table.

"Just messing with you. Have you ever watched the show *Bones*?"

"Seen it a few times."

Carol pointed at the book. "The author who wrote that was the inspiration for the main character."

Angie nodded. "Cool."

Carol had changed out of her blouse and slacks. It was a small shock to Angie, seeing her boss in faded jeans and a loose-fitting Rolling Stones t-shirt, her posture looser, more relaxed than at work.

She also held something in her hand — a rolled-up bundle tied in place by a frayed piece of white ribbon.

"What's that?" Angie said.

Carol came through the space between the couch and recliner and sat in the chair, with her butt perched on the very edge. "This," she said, "is the reason I had you come over."

She untied the ribbon and unrolled the bundle, unfolded it twice, then held it up at two ends for Angie to see. It was a large patchwork quilt that looked like it would easily cover a king-sized bed. The fabric was cream colored, but on each square was a multitude of single stitches, done with a silky black thread, which, at first glance, gave the impression of a thick swarm of flies.

"Have you ever seen one of these before?"

Angie furrowed her brow slightly. "A quilt? Um, yeah, I've seen them from time to time."

"Not just a quilt, Angie. One-hundred percent Amish stitch work. I dare you to look at it and find a single thread out of place."

Angie took a closer look. The quilt had indeed been crafted with care; on closer inspection, she saw the black stitches weren't randomly scattered, but occurred at the same points on each square. The longer she looked, the more they seemed to form an image.

A face.

"What's that picture on all the squares?"

Carol shook her head. "I have no earthly idea. Believe me, I've tried to figure it out, but I always come up blank. All I know is, from what you've told me, you could use some help getting to the truth. This quilt will get you there."

Angie looked up. "Huh?"

Carol lowered the quilt so that it covered her lap. "You know that I got divorced three years ago, right?

"Sure," Angie said.

"Do you know anything more than that?"

She shook her head, not mentioning the theories provided by the gossipier members of the warehouse crew.

"Well, the time leading up to it was … a rough time for me, just like you're having now. Maybe more so. Craig was a lot better at covering his tracks than your Ryan seems to be. But, after a while, he got sloppy. One night, I came home earlier than usual. I walked in on him in bed, playing with himself in front of his laptop."

Angie cringed and said, "Gross."

"Yes, it was. But I suppose you have to expect something like that at some point. Men get bored easy, as we know. If it had stopped at him diddling to porn, I might have kicked him out of bed for the night, but I'd have let it go before long." Her eyes drifted downward. "Except it didn't stop at that. Before I walked in, I heard him talking to someone, and when I opened the door, the first thing he did was shove something under his pillow."

She paused.

Angie gave her a knowing look. "His phone."

Carol nodded. "It couldn't have been anything else. I didn't let on that I suspected anything, and the next night, while Craig was asleep, I took his phone out of his pants pocket and looked through it. And … nothing. No unfamiliar numbers, no calls or texts, except for what he'd made to me, work, friends, et cetera."

"And let me guess. That just made you more suspicious."

Carol's face scrunched up, creating wrinkles on her nose. "Yep. So, the next thing I did was take his laptop in the kitchen and hack into his e-mail."

"You know how to hack a computer?"

"You can hack anyone who uses the same password for everything. I'm pretty sure he expected it, though. Same story as his phone: no suspicious e-mails or instant messages. But, oh lucky me, he hadn't thought to delete his site history. I brought it up and clicked to the last page he'd been to. All of a sudden I'm on a site called allbymyself.com, looking at some skinny, naked college boy jerking off while sucking on a giant dildo."

"Holy shit," Angie said.

There was now a bitter glare in Carol's eyes. "So, that was one mystery solved. The next thing I wondered was, who was he talking to on the phone?" She paused and took a breath. "I don't suppose I have to tell you it would have done no good to confront him. He'd have just said I was imagining things or that he got to that porn site by accident. So, there I am with my hands empty, I don't know for sure what's going on, and I need to spill it out to someone. Sound familiar?"

Angie raised an eyebrow and looked off to her side.

"So, that night," Carol continued, "I drove up to Shaw Station. My sister lives there. We went out and got drunk, and I told her everything. I was nowhere near sober enough to care who else heard it, and I get a tap on my shoulder, turn around, and there's a little old Amish lady standing there, vodka and cranberry in her hand, saying she couldn't help overhearing. Saying she wanted to help me."

"An Amish lady in a bar?"

"Sounds like the start of a bad joke, doesn't it? She was off work for the day and waiting for her ride home to show up. Turned out she owns Quilted Dreams on Main Street in Shaw Station. She makes all the quilts and candles there, handmade soap, everything. Mary-Ann Raber was her name. Anyway, I asked her, 'How the hell can you help me?' She tells me to give her my address and I'd find out. I was about six beers deep at that point, and I figured, what's the harm? It wasn't like I was giving her my social security number, and I doubted she belonged to some Amish burglary ring. So I wrote it down on a napkin for her.

"A few days later, this quilt shows up, Fed-Exed to my door. I open it, unfold it, and out falls a note from Mary-Ann, telling me to put this on my bed and sleep under it with Craig. She said the answers I wanted would 'come to me in my dreams'. I figured it was just some Amish superstition nonsense. I grew up in Shaw with them all around. They used to tell me stories about Braucha and all sorts of witchcraft they get into sometimes. Bunch of bull, if you had asked me then. But hey, this lady was nice enough to send me a free quilt. Why not humor her? Plus, it is damn comfy. So, I put it on the bed, and Craig and I slept under it that night."

"And what happened?"

There was a long moment of silence.

"I had a dream, that's what. Except, I wasn't me in the dream. I was Craig. I was seeing everything through his eyes, hearing what he heard. I was in our bathroom, sitting on the toilet seat lid. The shower was on, and I pulled my cell phone out of Craig's jeans and dialed a number. A man picked up, and I talked to him. Craig did, I mean. Craig was whispering, saying how much he missed him, wanted to see him." She closed her eyes and took a shaky breath. "How much he wanted to touch him. He told the man to send a picture. And he did, a selfie of himself laying shirtless on his bed. I saw his face. He was this … this scrawny little twenty-something kid. Long, black hair halfway to his shoulders. And Craig started to …"

Carol stopped and shook her head.

"He said a name a couple of times: Ben. Trying to keep his voice down the whole time. When he was done, he told Ben that he loved him and he'd see him soon, but he had to get back to that bitch in the living room. They said their goodbyes and hung up, and Craig deleted the call from his phone."

Carol took a slow breath in and out, blinking the tears and darkness away.

"And then I woke up. But I remembered everything, the phone number and the kid's face, his name. I don't suppose I need to tell you I didn't sleep the rest of the night.

"The next day, at work, I pulled my own phone out and called the number I'd seen in the dream. A man picked up. When I heard his voice, my whole body went cold. It was him, the same voice I'd heard in the dream. I said, 'Is this Ben?' It was quiet for a few seconds, and then he said, 'Who is this?' I hung up. I just sat there in my office, looking for any way to tell myself that this was all just a big misunderstanding, that Mary-Ann Raber was playing some sort of trick on me, or she'd put the dream there for some sick reason. I thought for a while and realized there was one more thing I could do. I pulled my phone out, brought up my Facebook app, and typed in the name 'Ben'. Of course, his face didn't pop right out at me. I had to scroll through a lot of Bens until I found him. But I found him."

"You saw his face?"

"Not just his face. The little faggot had changed his profile pic to the same photo he'd sent to Craig."

Angie's muscles tensed at the gay slur. She knew where it came from, though — hurt, not hate — and gave Carol a pass.

"So what did you do then?"

"What did I do? I locked my office door, grabbed my coat and bunched it up, and screamed into it as loud as I could, then I cried for about two hours. After that, this … it was weird, this coldness came over me. Or maybe relief. Shit, I don't know. But I wiped away the tears, went to the bathroom and washed my face off, and I went back to work. I worked my ass off that day. Actually, I think I might have gotten a little abrupt with you once or twice."

Angie didn't remember, and told her so. Carol cracked a little smile.

"I guess it couldn't have been that bad, then. After a while, the work day was over and it was time to go home. And, oh boy, the coldness wore off then. I pulled into the garage, and I was more scared of walking into my own house than I've ever been of anything. I must have sat in the car for a half hour. But, I made myself get out and go inside. I walked into the kitchen, and there was Craig, micro-waving a TV dinner. He said he thought I must have been working late and forgot to call. I didn't say anything, just walked up to him and held up my phone screen for him to look at."

Angie smiled. "You had the guy's picture up on your screen, didn't you?'

"Smart girl, Ange. And, sure enough, there was that look in his eye. I don't know how long it was, but we just stood there, not saying anything. Then he said 'Just let me grab some things to take with me tonight, and I'll get the rest later'."

Carol locked eyes with Angie and shrugged.

"And that is the story of my divorce."

Angie didn't speak. She started to several times, but couldn't find what she wanted to ask or say.

"The worst part is the not knowing, isn't it, Ange? Not knowing if you can trust him, trust your own instincts? Not knowing if any-thing is real between the two of you, or if it ever has been?"

Angie's lips parted, then closed. She nodded.

Carol lifted the quilt again, with one hand this time.

"As Mick and Keith might say, this might not give you the answers you want, but you might just find the ones that you need."

Angie's eyes moved from Carol's face down to the cream-colored quilt. She reached out with one hand and let her fingers touch the soft fabric.

Chapter 3

Ryan surprised Angie by being awake and on the couch when she got home, and then again by smiling as she stood in the doorway. He closed the issue of "Blood Binge Magazine" he was reading, set it on the arm of the couch, then swung his legs off the cushions and sat up straight.

"Hey, stranger," he said.

"Hey," Angie replied, making no attempt at warmth.

Ryan rubbed his hands. "What'cha got there?"

He nodded at the quilt, which Angie held under her right arm, rolled up and tied with the white ribbon.

Angie herself had been wondering that same thing. Driving home, she'd realized just how nuts that whole story sounded, wondered if Carol had recently been hitting the sauce a little hard. After all, magic quilts and dreams where you saw through someone else's eyes? That shit didn't happen.

"Gift from Carol," she said.

"Ah. Looks comfy."

"Mm."

Ryan patted the couch cushion his feet had just been on.

"Why don't you toss that on the bed and come back in here. We can have a little talk time. Haven't done that in a while."

Angie inhaled slowly, blinked a few times, and turned back into the hallway. She hurled the quilt, underhand, through the bedroom door, landing it on the floor next to her side of the bed, and went back to the living room.

She hesitated when she got to the couch. Ryan had switched positions again and now sat cross-legged, looking up at Angie with puppy dog eyes.

"Please?" he said.

She looked down at him, and her chest trembled. In that moment, she didn't see Ryan the Liar or Ryan the Possible Cheat. She saw the gawky, nerdy Ryan Berg she was sure she knew until recently.

Her Ryan.

Stay cold, she told herself.

She sat down at the other end of the couch, foot tucked under her leg, and looked at Ryan with what she hoped was a stare of indifference.

"So?" she prodded.

Ryan opened his palms outward. "So. Did you read the messages I sent you?"

"I was working."

Ryan nodded and looked down for a second, seeming to catch

on he would have his work cut out.

Good.

"Well, I'm sorry about last night. That's what I said in them. And that's what I want to say to you now."

"That's all you want to say? You're sorry?"

"I shouldn't have blown up like that. I won't try to make excuses, except to say I was only half awake when I saw you."

"Yeah? You sure seemed wide awake when you jumped up and snatched your phone out of my hand."

Ryan spread his palms. "I thought you were snooping, and I just kind of lost it, I guess."

"The battery on my phone died while I was paying the internet bill. I was just going to use yours to get back with them. I wasn't snooping."

"I know. I know that now."

"Besides, why would you get so upset about me looking at your phone? Was there something on there you didn't want me to see?"

Ryan looked her in the eyes, dead serious. "No. Nothing."

The screen saver flashed through Angie's mind.

"Look." He pulled his phone from his pajama pants pocket and held it up in front of Angie. "Here. If you want, you can go through it right now. Look at anything you want. There's nothing I'm trying to keep from you."

Angie looked at the phone.

And, nothing. No unfamiliar numbers.

"No, I'm good. So, then, why did you freak out?"

Ryan sighed, returned the phone to his pocket. "Just because ... I don't like people sneaking through my stuff. My mom used to do it to me all the time, go through my closet and shit. It's a sore spot with me, that's all."

Angie looked for any trace of deceit in his face, any flick of his eyes away from her. There was none, as far as she could see. She leaned her elbow against the back of the couch and tilted her head sideways, resting it in the palm of her hand. "What about the past few weeks, Ryan? What's up with that? Used to be I would get home from work and you'd be wide awake, all rested up. Now, I get home and you're in the bedroom, still asleep. You don't wake up until it's almost time for you to go to the hospital. Would you maybe care to explain that?"

Ryan looked down at the hardwood floor, shook his head, and shrugged. "I wish I could," he said. "I mean, you've worked thirds before. You know how it is. You get home and can't get to sleep one morning, and that ends up being how the whole week or month goes. Trust me, if it were up to me, I'd be up and waiting for you every day, and I'd sit here with my arms around you all evening ..."

"Stop trying to butter me up, Ryan."

"Okay, fair enough. Point is, you take somebody's brain and make them readjust to all sorts of weird hours, the pattern gets messed up and sleep just comes when it wants to."

"Uh-huh." Angie wanted to believe him, but there was still the matter of the screen saver. She'd only seen it for a second before Ryan snatched the phone away, but the image was still branded in her mind.

The girl couldn't have been more than twenty. She had long, dark brown hair and features that made her look vaguely feline. There had been a blank and wide-eyed expression on her face, as though whoever took the picture had yelled "Hey! Over here!" and caught her off guard.

The girl in the picture was the one loose end. Like Carol Drake before her, Angie had scrolled through all three hundred plus of Ryan's Facebook friends, looking for anyone who resembled the girl. She'd come up dry.

She wondered now, was it possible her mind had played a trick on her? That, somewhere down the line, her brain took a snapshot of a girl at Wal-Mart, or in a passing car, and she'd stored it in her subconscious and pasted it on Ryan's phone screen last night, just to play on fears she didn't even know she had?

... you could use some help getting to the truth. This quilt will get you there

...

Fuck it, she thought. *What could it hurt?*

She said, "Okay, then. I forgive you."

A smile spread across Ryan's face.

"On one condition."

Ryan nodded. "Anything."

Angie slid herself closer to him, took his hand in hers, and squeezed it tight. "You still have some emergency vacation days left, don't you?"

Ryan shrugged. "A few. Remember, you wanted me to save them

for the winter when the roads got bad?"

"Well, screw that. I want you to take tonight off and spend it with me."

She paid attention to his face, looking for hesitation. Instead, she saw relief. She hoped it was because She-Forgives-Me, not She-Believes-Me.

"I do that, and we'll be cool?"

Angie raised an eyebrow. "You make it sound like a chore."

Ryan shook his head. "Never a chore to start the weekend early, especially if I get to spend it with you. Tell you what, I'll call the hospital and tell them I got a cold. Not allowed to work if you got something contagious."

"Are they going to be mad?"

"Hey, push comes to shove, the nurses can empty their own fucking wastebaskets."

Angie smiled and squeezed his hand. He squeezed back. The familiarity of his weak grip made her heart stir a little. She hoped that after tonight she'd have her skinny, little nerd back.

They spent the evening on the couch. Ryan had picked up Chinese food, and they ate and caught up on the last few episodes of *Bates Motel*, then streamed a couple of cheesy horror movies on Netflix.

Angie lay on the couch with her head on Ryan's chest, wearing gray sweat pants and a tank top, no bra underneath. There were a few times she considered grabbing his hand and placing it on her breast, letting him massage it the way he did when he wanted to let her know he was horny. It was clear, though, from the way he rubbed his eyes and yawned constantly, there'd be no fireworks tonight.

They went into the bedroom around eleven and slid under the quilt, which Angie had replaced the plush comforter with while Ryan was picking up dinner.

"This is a lot comfier than it looks," Ryan said, yawning and pulling the edge of the quilt to his chin.

"One hundred percent Amish stitch work," Angie parroted. She lay on her side, facing Ryan. He turned his head toward her. "I'm happy things are okay with us, now."

"Me, too."

"And I swear, I'm not going to be asleep anymore when you get home, okay? I don't want us to be that couple that drifts away from each other and ends up living together like a couple of strangers."

Angie threw her arm over his shoulders. "Me neither. But I know it sucks working thirds, too, so maybe I'll cut you some slack if you need to sleep in sometimes."

"Deal."

She leaned over and kissed him, letting it last a long time and, just this once, she gave him a break and used her tongue. Afterward, she laid her head on her pillow, but kept her hand on his chest until he passed out a few minutes later.

She turned the light out on her side of the bed. Closing her eyes, she was certain the picture on his phone had been a misunderstanding. That Ryan was still her Ryan. And she knew that she wouldn't be seeing any other woman in her dreams tonight.

And if she did, the slut would be dead when she saw her.

Chapter 4

In the dream, she is him.

Straw-colored grass crunches beneath her footsteps. Through the glare of the morning sun, a crumbling barn drifts toward her like an iceberg.

There is a noise in the distance. She turns and looks at the country road beyond the dilapidated house, prepared to rush and duck behind a nearby rusted tractor when, across the road, she sees a lone deer run through the cut-down cornfield.

No sound of cars coming. She turns back and continues on.

She swings the barn door open slowly, one creak at a time. The reek of old shit and dry rot escapes from inside. She steps in, slams the door shut, making it bang.

Muffled whimpers and a dry sniffle come from the far corner of the barn. Hearing them, she moves her fingers to her crotch and strokes gently through her pants, then walks toward the noise.

She passes empty stables and comes to the last one, which is boarded up into a room of its own, with a door made from a large piece of plywood, with a rope handle midway up. She pulls it open and walks into the pitch blackness.

There are moans and pleading. She kneels down to a backpack sitting just inside the door, unzips it and fishes out a halogen lantern, flips it on.

In the harsh glow of the lamp, she sees the girl, face-down on a ratty and torn mattress, covered by a navy blue blanket.

She walks to the bed, bringing the backpack with her, grabs one corner of the blanket and tugs it slowly away from the girl, exposing her bare shoulder blades and bound arms. The girl's wrists are cuffed behind her with three zip ties, one on each wrist and one holding them together.

She retrieves a long leather belt from the backpack, and a plastic container from a smaller compartment. It makes a rattling sound as she shoves it in her pocket.

She stands back up with the lamp in one hand, belt in the other, holds the lantern in front of the girl. Moves the light over her body. Examines the welts. The girl's buttocks and thighs have gotten the worst of it.

She holds the belt out, lets the strap dangle down, and lowers the tip of it onto the small of the girl's back, then drags it slowly and gently across her flesh. The girl hyperventilates and sobs; she pleads through the strip of duct tape covering her mouth.

Though the girl's words are muffled, their meaning is clear: Please, no more.

She is breathing hard now. He lifts the belt off her and steps away and sets the lantern down on the floor. The light makes monstrous shadows. She wraps the leather strap around her hand until it is rolled up all the way, then returns it to the backpack. She kneels beside the girl and brushes her shoulder with her fingers. The girl recoils.

"Hey," she says in a baritone voice not her own, but instantly recognizable. "Hey, it's okay. There won't be any of that today."

The girl trembles and sucks snot into her nose.

"It's okay to cry. I know this is hard for you. If you're hungry, I got some peanut butter crackers I brought with me. Do you want some?"

It takes the girl a moment, but she shakes her head no.

"Okay, well, you should really eat something soon. And next time I come here, I'll see about bringing some water and shampoo and all that, and we'll get you cleaned up. How does that sound?"

The girl gives no response.

"All right. Well, like I said, no belt today."

She reaches one hand over the girl's waist. Rolls her over, nurse-like. Tears have made the tape start to come loose from the girl's eyes.

"Here. There's no point in having this on."

She peels the rest of the tape away and pulls the wrapped-around strip off the girl's head.

"Now, listen. There is something I do have to do today."

She reaches into her pocket, pulls out the plastic container. She looks down at the girl's smallish breasts, takes one of the soft nipples between her thumb and forefinger, pinches and tugs lightly until it begins to harden and stick out.

She looks up and into the girl's puffy red eyes. They are dazed and half dead, but possess the slightest glimmer of something still alive, deep down.

She pops the top off the container and pulls out one of the safety pins.

"I just want you to know this has nothing to do with you. You haven't done anything wrong, okay?"

The girl's eyes meet the pin and her body quakes as though in seizure.

She pulls a lighter from the same pocket she pulled the container from, unfastens the safety pin, strikes the lighter. She holds the pin still, lifts the flame up to the needle point, and slides the tip of it up and down the thin metal.

"See, I've thought of everything. The heat will keep the bleeding down. It'll be just like getting your ears pierced."

The girl's screams are taking their toll on her throat, and she stops once in a while, coughing and wheezing through her nostrils, then screams more.

She releases her thumb from the lighter and sets it on the floor.

"Okay, I need you to be real still for me okay. I don't want to scratch you up or tear you."

She pinches the nipple, which has lost some of its hardness, plays with it until it hardens again. She pulls it upward, stretching out the top layer of flesh. The girl's cries have died down to sporadic squeaks.

"Okay," she says in a barely audible whisper. "Okay."

Chapter 5

Angie woke, and in the dark she felt like she'd been blindfolded and spun around twenty times. Despite the bed beneath her, she couldn't figure out which way was up or down, which side was right or left.

"Angie. Hey."

She shrieked and sat up. A hand grabbed her shoulder.

"Angie, Angie, hey, calm down."

She looked over. Ryan was sitting up beside her.

He said, "You had a nightmare."

He slid his hand from her shoulder to her neck and began to massage it gently. Angie's arms tensed up and her knees came together, tight.

"It was just a dream, Ange. You okay?"

Angie tried to get out the one simple word 'Yeah', but it stuck in her chest. She nodded instead, sniffled, and noticed the tears drying on her cheeks.

"Are you sure?"

Ryan ran the tips of his fingers up and down her spine. It was what she liked him to do while they watched TV, with Angie resting her head on his stomach, sometimes falling asleep from the sensation. Now, all she could think of was the tip of the leather belt dragging across the girl's back.

"I'm okay. Just a bad dream."

"What about?"

She looked over at him and saw an expression that told her he was listening. But, in the dark to which her eyes had adjusted, and with his fingers sliding along the fabric of her shirt, it seemed as though there were something else in his face.

Or rather, an absence of something.

No, she told herself. *That's dumb. It was just a bad dream. Magic quilts don't exist, and husbands don't torture girls.*

"Angie?"

"I, uh ... I can't remember. Just a dream."

Goddamn right, it was just a dream.

Her body remained tense and alert, though, especially to Ryan's hand, which was still on her back, his whole palm flat against it.

"Poor girl. It's all good, now. You're safe and sound."

His hand slid under her shirt, and his fingers brushed against the skin of her lower back. A shiver ran through her and pushed goose-bumps up on her arms.

"Jesus. You are clenched all the way up, aren't you?"

Angie forced a laugh. "I just need a second to relax and I'll be fine. You go on and go back to sleep. I have to pee, anyway."

She wasn't lying. Her bladder was about to explode, and when she made it to the bathroom and pulled her pajama pants down, she saw there was a small wet dot in the crotch of her underwear.

"Fuck."

After relieving herself, she went to the laundry room at the back of the house and exchanged her wet panties for a pair of dry ones from the hamper — not clean, but dry. She made her way through the kitchen and down the hall. In the bedroom, a light had been turned on. She halted, reluctant to go toward it.

Why? It's just Ryan in there. Ryan, your skinny, little nerd, the man you've shared a bed with — when he has the night off — for almost three years now. Nothing to be afraid of. A dream is just a dream, no matter what that crazy bitch Carol says. Did you notice how clean her house was? She probably doesn't sleep, just vacuums all night and wipes everything down with that yellow spray cleaner shit and the fumes have wrecked her brain.

For all her mental scrambling, Angie still stood at the end of the hallway, looking at the light. Sometimes, when Ryan worked nights and she was alone in the house, she'd hear some noise or other, and a picture would flash in her head of a stranger in a ski mask tiptoeing through the living room. She had that same feeling now, except the stranger was in her bed this time, waiting with some comment like 'Feeling better?'

She forced herself to take a step forward. The light in the doorway began to float toward her.

"Feeling better?" Ryan said.

Angie nodded and got under the quilt, trying to keep her breath steady. "Why'd you turn the light on?"

She looked at the design of the quilt to avoid Ryan's eyes.

"You seemed like you might be up for a while. I figured, since we're having a special weeknight together, I'd give you the famous Ryan Berg Backrub."

The thought of his hands on her again made her cringe inside. She told herself to stop, that there was no sense in this. And just to prove it ...

"Yeah. That sounds nice."

"Alrighty, then." He leaned over and kissed her on the neck. "Lay down and roll on over."

Somehow, Angie managed to crack a smile. "Does that line work with all the girls?"

Ryan laughed and pulled the quilt off Angie's body. She sat up and tossed her pillow to the floor beside her, then pulled her shirt over her head. She then lay back down, topless, and rolled over onto her stomach.

Normally, it was no big thing to have herself on display like this in front of Ryan. Not anymore, at least. Early in their courtship, when they first started to get physical, she'd feel the urge to cover herself so he wouldn't see her love handles, her little bit of belly flab. She grew less shy over time, as it became clear Ryan was aware of her perceived flaws but didn't seem to mind them. He even seemed to enjoy them, like when they would spoon in bed and he would hang his arm over her side and massage and caress her stomach. That weirded her out at first, but she grew used to it, even began to like it as she realized it was one of his odd little ways of showing affection.

Now, half naked in the light with Ryan, her body refused to relax. When his hands touched her back and dug gently into her muscles, her flesh writhed in protest.

Stop it, she thought. *It's just Ryan.* As though trying to calm a barking dog.

"You all right? You're really clenched up."

"I'm fine. Just a tough week at work." She realized it had come out more rushed than she'd intended.

"Well, just one more day, right?"

"Yeah."

His hands moved to her shoulders, then slid down her arms. He lowered his body onto hers. She felt the warmth of his bare stomach and chest against her back, and then the heat of his breath on her neck as he brushed her ear with the tip of his nose.

"Everything is okay between us, right?" His voice was low and smooth, almost a whisper.

"Y-Yeah, of course. It's all good."

She felt the wetness of his lips against her neck. He ran his hand down the side of her ass and squeezed her outer thigh.

"Good," he said. "I love you, you know. You and nobody else."

Angie opened her mouth, but no words formed in her mind. Instead, she nodded slightly.

Ryan's hand traveled back up to the top of her hip and slid into the waistband of her panties, his open palm moving lightly over her bare skin. Her knees moved closer together. Her vagina tightened and closed itself off. She felt her pajama pants and underwear being lowered as Ryan's lips moved from her neck to her shoulder.

"Why don't you turn on over?"

Angie didn't try to tell herself this was okay anymore. The arousal that Ryan's touch usually brought wasn't there tonight. There was no tingling in her breasts or between her legs. No wetness or hunger. There was only repulsion.

She turned over anyway.

They kissed, or rather she let him kiss her. His hand moved over her left breast. He took her nipple between his thumb and index finger, played with it. Against Angie's will, it stiffened and rose. In her mind she saw the same thing play out. Same hand, same movement of fingers, but on a different body.

As Ryan lowered himself down and dragged his tongue over her chest and stomach, all Angie could think of was the dragging of a belt.

Chapter 6

Her phone alarm went off as the sun began to shine through the bedroom window. She turned it off and took her ear buds out, set them on the table beside her phone, and returned to laying on her back, eyes half open, knowing that when she looked in the bathroom mirror, a baggy, pale face would be looking back.

After they finished making love — or rather, after Ryan finished while Angie pretended to — she tried to go back to sleep, thinking maybe she would dream again beneath the quilt, and it would be different this time. Maybe something bizarre and disjointed she'd only half remember. Maybe another nightmare, one that played out some other horrific scene, completely unrelated to the one before. At least then she could safely say it was her mind that was fucked up and not Ryan's.

But it didn't happen. She lay awake all night, Ryan sleeping beside her like the dead. When it was clear she wouldn't be joining him, she got her earbuds from the living room and plugged them into her phone. She brought up her iTunes playlist and listened to the ethereal beat of 'Melody's Echo Chamber', thinking in the dark the whole while.

There had to be some way of finding solid proof that the dream wasn't real.

Her first idea was to search Ryan's car and throughout the house for the backpack she'd seen. But then she remembered it had already been there, waiting in the barn.

Besides, not finding it wouldn't mean a damn thing.

Around four, it came to her — she had seen the girl in the dream, her face and hair. She remembered it as clearly as if she was right in front of her. Angie was certain she'd never seen that face before.

Except in the screen saver.

That piece of the puzzle dug into her the deepest. The girl in the dream was the same girl she saw on Ryan's phone the night before last. It had been swimming under the surface the whole time, and when it finally stuck its head out, Angie's stomach sunk.

The phone alarm went off again; Angie always set two alarms for the morning, fifteen minutes apart. Ryan stirred at her side and rolled over to face her.

"Gonna turn that off?"

He sounded like his usual grumpy morning self. Angie turned off the alarm, turned her head, and saw that he'd shut his eyes again. He wasn't asleep, though — he'd lay there awake until the grogginess had worn off, and then he'd get up to pee and make coffee.

Angie got an idea. She turned on her side with her back to Ryan, placed her phone on the mattress close to her, brought up her Google app and typed in "missing persons Indiana."

One site linked her to a page where she had to click on the first three letters of a missing person's last name, which linked her to another page where she had to click on one of the names that came up just to see that person's photo and info. The other sites were no better, none of them offering a way to just scroll through various photos. Even the FBI's "kidnapped and missing persons" section seemed to cherry pick who went on the list.

She found one last site, a community page on good old Facebook, where people could post info and pics of their missing loved ones. Apparently, she wasn't the only one who'd noticed the other sites didn't have their shit together.

Prepared to come up empty-handed yet again, Angie clicked the link that would take her to the page.

And there was the girl.

It was the most recent post on the wall, only a few weeks old. There was a video link pasted there, the paused frame showing the girl in a booth at a restaurant, smiling and holding a sandwich in her hands, a book beside her tray. There was life and light in her eyes, color in her cheeks, and her hair was washed and flowing. Nothing like the condition the girl in the dream had been in, but it was her.

Angie read the text that ran below the video:

> My daughter, Amy Moore, never came home
> last Friday. She was last seen riding her bike
> home from the Marathon gas station on US 31

between Westfield and Kokomo. She was wearing jeans and a green-and-gold Westfield Shamrocks t-shirt. She is seventeen years old, has long, dark brown hair, green eyes, weighs 104 pounds, and is 5'1". Please, if you have any information, contact the Westfield Police Department.

Angie looked back at the frozen video. She grabbed her ear buds off the nightstand and put them in, lifted her finger to the screen. Her finger hovered a moment above Amy Moore's face, then she pressed the "Play" button.

The person taking the video sat down across from her. A male voice spoke. "So, here today, we have an exclusive interview with bestselling author, Ms. Amy Moore."

Amy, chewing a bite of grilled chicken sandwich, rolled her eyes and smiled.

"Yeah. Riiight," she said, doing an impression of Dr. Evil.

"Miz Moore, how does it feel to go from humble beginnings to being a published writer?"

Amy swallowed before talking. "You mean how does it feel to get a two-page short story published on a fantasy site no one's heard of?"

Holding a fry, she looked out the window for a few seconds, then burst into a smile and looked back at the camera. "It's the best feeling I've ever had." She popped the fry into her mouth.

"I'm proud of you, honey," the male voice said. "So, tell us what your story's about."

Amy wagged her finger. "Mm-mm, no spoilers! You have to wait for it to come out, and then you can see."

"Oh, come on, you're gonna torture your dad for that long? Are you that sadistic?"

"Yes, I am. Ha-ha-ha!"

"Come on! Please tell me?"

Amy let out a dramatic sigh. "Oh, fine!"

Her smiled waned a bit, and she looked down at her tray, stirring a fry in a puddle of ketchup.

"It's about a mother and her little girl who've gotten into a car accident. They slid off the road and crashed into these woods. It's winter, and they're way out in the country. The car is upside down. The mother crawls into the backseat with her little girl — the girl is strapped in her car seat — and they have to wait through the whole night for someone to come along and get help. When they do, they come and rescue the little girl, take her out of the backseat, and get her to someplace warm. The mother is still in the backseat, and she looks up at the front seat and sees herself there. The reader finds out she died in the crash, but she remained as a ghost so her little girl wouldn't be alone. And the story ends with the mother smiling and this light forming all around her, taking her to heaven."

Amy pursed her lips, then looked back down and took a bite of the fry she'd been stirring the whole while. "And that's it."

The man holding the camera was silent for long moment before saying, "You're a hell of a girl, hon."

She nodded and looked up with narrowed eyes. "I know."

"Love you."

Amy covered her face in mock embarrassment, and then looked at the camera. "Love you, too."

The screen went black and up came the frozen frame of the start of the video.

Ryan breathed deeply behind Angie and let out a soft groan. She exited the page and brought her phone back to her home screen. Her lungs hurt as she tried to keep her breathing normal and quiet.

Angie knew where Westfield was. She and Ryan had driven through it on U.S. 31 while making their way down to Indy last year for Horror Hound Weekend. It was about a half hour north of the city and the last suburb you hit before the landscape turned into flat country. She remembered passing that gas station. What was it, a two, two and a half hour drive from here?

Jesus Christ! An image popped into her head: Ryan driving north on 31 with Amy Moore, bound and gagged, on the floor of the backseat.

Angie shut her eyes and forced the picture from her mind. There was a hot stirring in her stomach, and she felt last night's Chinese food circling upwards into her throat. She covered her mouth, tightened her esophagus, and made a fist with her right hand, digging her nails into the flesh of her palm. After several minutes, the nausea gave up, but by no means went away.

The phone alarm went off again. She jumped, and a high shriek came from her mouth. A hand touched her shoulder, making her jump again.

"Angie, what the hell's the matter?"

She turned and looked at Ryan, who was rubbing the sleep from his eyes with his free hand.

She said, "Still jumpy, I guess. More bad dreams after I went back to sleep."

Ryan nodded, but there was still a look of concern in his eyes. Angie realized what was causing it as she became aware of her mouth hanging open and her eyes peeled wide.

"Maybe you should take the day off, yourself," Ryan said. "As many hours as you've been working, that's probably what this all is. Catching up to you, you know?"

Angie tried to smile, but what she managed was closer to a grimace. "Yeah, well, it sucks, but ... all part of being one of the higher-ups, right? No, I'll ... I'll be fine. Friday anyway, right?"

Ryan lightly squeezed the flesh of her arm. "Alright. Suit yourself. Tell you what. You lie in here and get calmed down, and I'll make some coffee and whip up a couple pieces of French toast. You still got time, right?"

"Yeah. Um, you know what? I'm actually going to take a shower while you do all that. Nightmare sweats made me all gross."

Ryan laughed. "Alright. You do that, and I'll have everything ready in the kitchen when you're done. Just let me pee before you get in there, though."

* * *

Everything was amplified as Angie got in the shower: the sliding of the curtain rings along the rod; the creak of the knob as she lifted and turned it; and the spray of hot water that landed on her skin. The heat sent a small shock wave through her system, but she leaned into it, closed her eyes. She wanted nothing more than to lie down and curl up and fall asleep in the warm rain.

How was she going to deal with this? He was out there right now. Making French fucking toast.

She'd seen a movie once about a woman who finds out her husband is a killer who murders women while away on business. Angie couldn't recall how the story went, exactly, except that the wife kills her husband, then finds out the police were closing in on him the whole time.

Maybe the police were closing in on Ryan, too. Maybe, after she left for work, he'd decide to take a trip out to that old barn, and the police would be following. They'd take him to the ground when they found the girl, slap the handcuffs on before he had a chance to do anything else to Amy Moore. Maybe Angie had to do nothing but wait.

Or maybe you're just wishing in one hand. Now, try shitting in the other.

Angie realized she was just standing there under the shower head. She grabbed her blue, rose-shaped lather sponge from where it hung on the knob, squeezed some of her body wash on it, and rubbed the lather on her chest and arms, its butterscotch scent drifting up to her nose.

No, if that girl was going to be saved before Ryan killed her —

either going too far in his sick games, or because he was tired of her and wanted a new girl to play with — then Angie would have to be the catalyst.

The obvious answer was to go to the police and tell them everything she knew.

Which is what? she thought. *That your boss's magic quilt made you dream about your husband holding a girl captive in a barn? That you saw her photo on Facebook and decided yep, that's her? Are you going to show them the screen saver on Ryan's phone? The one you mistook for a selfie but was probably a pic of her, scared and in pain, that he likely took to get himself hard in the bathroom before he has to go hump that fat, boring wife of his? Go ahead. After all, it's a given he'll still have it on his phone after that close call the other night. And when the cops ask you where they can find that torture barn, what are you going to tell them? There's no GPS on Ryan's car, no computer in that old POS, so what are you going to tell them? Hmm? Where's the barn, Ange?*

She lowered her aching head and closed her eyes. "Shit."

The water from the shower head began to lose heat and went from scalding to warm. Angie rinsed herself and reached for the shampoo. She scoured her mind and memory for any clues, tried to remember anything Ryan might have told her once about a place in the country, maybe somewhere he used to go as a kid.

She came up with nothing.

That was all fantasy bullshit, anyway, the idea that everything was tied together by a convenient little bow. More likely, Ryan had just happened upon the place one day while driving in the country and decided it would do.

Angie rinsed the shampoo out of her hair and switched to conditioner, trying to think of some plan.

Then, a plan burst into her mind, fully formed the way some ideas do.

She would pretend to go to work for the day, like always, then find a spot nearby where she could park and watch the house, and hope Ryan decided to take a trip to the barn. If and when he did, she would follow behind him at a far enough distance to not be noticed. When he arrived at the farm, she would let him go into the stable, where he wouldn't see outside, and then pass by the house and get its address. She'd park down the road, call the police, and report a trespasser on the land. It would take a minute for them to arrive — traipsing through abandoned barns was probably not their highest priority. If Ryan had left by the time they got there, she would just have to satisfy herself, at least for the time being, that they'd find the girl and get her the hell out of there.

Angie sighed at the whole plan. She wasn't thrilled by the idea of playing detective and hero. This wasn't some damn fairytale. The girl in the barn wasn't a damsel in distress locked in a tower; she was a girl who'd done nothing wrong, but was nevertheless trapped in a dark and smelly place, suffering and scared.

And the man who'd put her there? He wasn't some comic book villain with a twirling mustache.

He was Ryan.

Her Ryan.

Or so she'd once thought.

Angie rinsed the conditioner from her hair, then remained in the shower for some time. She let the now-cold water freeze and punish her skin until she shook and closed her eyes.

The tears started to flow.

For the first time since this whole thing had started, she let them.

When she finally emerged from the bathroom, she was wrapped in a pale blue towel that barely went past the top of her legs.

Standing in the hallway, looking down into the kitchen, she noticed there was no smell of coffee or French toast. And it was way too quiet.

A dull nervousness flared up in her.

She only heard a few quick footsteps before she felt the blow against the back of her head, and darkness flooded in as the floor came up to meet her.

Chapter 7

She woke up face down in pitch darkness, soreness pulsing in her head.

The surface beneath her was lumpy and reeked of urine and mold. Her arms were bound behind her, so she couldn't turn. She knew where she was, though, and a pinball of sickness bounced in her stomach.

Her eyes adjusted, and she made out the silhouette of a human figure lying beside her on the bed. The urine smell was coming from that direction. There was another odor beneath it, one that Angie didn't recognize and wasn't sure she wanted to.

"Amy?" She kept her voice low, almost at a whisper.

The girl didn't respond.

Angie tried lifting her head to look around. The room spun, and her eyelids got heavy. She dropped her head back down.

No, no, no, no. Keep with it, Ange.

She looked at the girl again. "Amy, please tell me you're awake."

"I don't think you'll get much out of her."

Angie jerked toward the direction of the voice. Pain exploded in her head again. She opened her mouth to cry out, but no sound came. She lay there with her face tight and twisted.

The room lit up, filling her eyes with unbearable whiteness. She shut them until the white faded to red. When she opened her eyes again, she could see semi-clearly the stained mattress beneath her, and the plywood floor beyond.

She looked beside her and into Amy Moore's open, lifeless eye — and screamed.

A pair of black and red tennis shoes appeared in her line of sight. Khaki-covered legs bent down into a squat. There was a hand on her shoulder, then Angie felt herself rolled onto her back.

She saw Ryan's face upside-down. He held something out in front of her.

Her phone.

"You always do keep your earbuds on full blast. Guess you didn't hear me sit up when you were watching that video of her."

Angie remained silent.

"Now, listen to me. I didn't kill her, okay? You have to believe me. We got here and she was just … gone. Maybe it was dehydration, or …" He shrugged and shook his head. "I don't know, maybe I was too rough on her."

Angie looked at Amy Moore again, saw the safety pins in her torso and legs. Little spots of dried blood were caked around the wounds. She looked at her face. Amy had died with a blank expression, and it occurred to Angie that perhaps nothing had killed her, exactly. Maybe she'd just given up the will to live.

Tears pooled in her eyes. She convulsed and began vomiting.

"Shit," Ryan said. He turned her onto her side, away from the corpse, and stroked her hair as she emptied her stomach. When she was done, she began sobbing.

"Why, Ryan? Why did you do it?" She spoke through tears, almost incoherent.

"I told you, I didn't kill her."

"Yes, you did, you son of a bitch."

"NO!" Ryan stood up and stepped back. "I was going to let her go, Angie."

She shook her head. "Bullshit."

Ryan stayed silent and still for a moment, then walked around the bed, stepping over the pool of puke. He knelt down beside the work lamp, opened the side pocket of the backpack, and fished something out.

"I was going to give her these." He held up two full vials where she could see them. "Propofol and liquid Lorazepam. Combine them together, and it creates a hypnotic state in a person. Makes them really suggestive. You have to be really careful, though; this is the same combo that killed Michael Jackson. When I was done with her, I was going to stick these in her and spend a day, you know, messing around in her head so she wouldn't remember anything when I let her go."

He looked intently at Angie. "It was as much for her as for me."

"Oh, was it now?"

"I guess, in a way, it's a good thing she didn't make it. I mean, I can't swipe these from the hospital just whenever, right? Now I can use them on you."

An icy chill ran through Angie. She imagined herself strapped to a dentist-like chair in a dark room, a strobe light flashing while Ryan spoke calm suggestions in a soft monotone. It wouldn't be like that for real — he couldn't afford that kind of setup — but he had something like that planned for her.

"It's the only way we can make this right," he continued. "I should've done it the other night, but I guess I chickened out."

Angie shut her eyes. How the hell was she going to get out of this? Ryan was clearly far gone. She opened her eyes and saw her husband stick the needle into the first vial. *This,* she thought, *must be what it's like to be a death row prisoner strapped to the injection chair.*

Then her thoughts scattered as the needle stung her upper arm. She turned her head toward the pain and saw the needle penetrating her flesh. A cloud of red displaced the clear fluid within the syringe.

Acting without thinking, she jerked her body, trying to roll onto her side. The motion caused the needle to tear free from her arm. Blood spurted, and shockwaves of pain ran through her. Ryan lost his grip on the syringe and it fell to the floor, shattering.

"Oh, God!" Ryan, still on his knees, grabbed a fistful of his own hair. "Oh, my God! What the fuck did you do?"

Angie lay silent.

"What the fuck did you do? Stupid bitch!"

He threw his fist into Angie's rib cage. She shrieked. Ryan pulled his arm back for another go, but stopped himself.

"No, it's okay. It's okay. Angie, it's all going to be all right. I'm … I'm sorry I hit you." He caressed her trembling side. "I promise that'll never happen again. But, now, I have to … I guess I'll have to go get some more, that's all."

He was talking to himself now. "Just go back to the hospital, say I forgot something. No big deal. It's all going to be okay." He stood up and spoke to Angie. "You'll see, it's all going to be fine."

Angie heard the door swing open, Ryan's footsteps getting fainter and fainter until there was the far-off sound of a door being opened and shut.

Angie tried repeatedly to roll herself over, but only succeeded in robbing herself of her strength and making her sides cramp and burn. Exhausted, she lay on her stomach for what seemed like hours, re-cover and trying not to contemplate what would happen when Ryan returned.

A deep despair washed over her. She turned her head toward the girl once more and said, "I'm sorry."

Then, looking at the girl, something began forming in Angie's mind. She tried to put her finger on it. Something to do with the safety pins cruelly marking Amy's body.

Then the idea seemed to burst forth, fully formed, into her head. A possible light in the tunnel. It would be hard, and horrific, and who knew how much longer she had before her husband came back? But she had to try.

She started moving her hips, legs, and shoulders, trying to gain traction. After a few minutes, she felt her body move slightly along the surface of the filthy mattress. This little bit of friction ignited a fire in Angie, and she wiggled twice as hard, scooting herself closer to Amy, bit by bit. At last, her elbow bumped against the girl's cold flesh.

Angie shuddered at what she had to do next. She tried her best to force all emotion from her mind as she scooted down until her head was level with Amy's lower torso.

Angie steeled herself further, then craned her neck and extended it as far as it would go. She lowered her mouth over one of the pins in Amy's side, clamped her teeth over it, and pulled it free from the dead layer of skin with sickening ease. She yanked her head away and spat out the pin onto the mattress between the two of them.

After scooting back up to where she was level with Amy's head, Angie used every ounce of strength left in her to twist to her side and reach the pin with her bound right hand. After much fumbling around, she managed to snag it between her pinkie and ring fingers. It dangled precariously as she brought her arms back to rest above her tailbone. She dropped the pin onto her back, and then picked it back up with her thumb and forefinger.

Shaking, Angie jabbed herself several times while attempting to locate the clasp of the zip tie on her left wrist. She took a moment to clear her mind, willing herself to ignore the adrenaline, taking deep breaths in and out.

She stilled her body enough to slide the pin inside the clasp of the tie. She pushed up, freeing the ridges, and shoved the pin the rest of the way through so it held the lock open.

She pulled out the slack and her wrist came free.

Just in time!

She heard the barn door open and close. Footsteps approached the room.

Angie turned herself over and sat up. She unlocked the zip tie around her left ankle, her movements now sure and confident.

The plywood door began to open.

The tie came loose and Angie was free.

No longer feeling pain in her head or arm — only adrenaline and feral rage — she jumped up and ran across the small room as Ryan's face appeared in the doorway. She jumped and slammed into the door, swinging it outward. The edge of the door hit Ryan in the face and knocked him on his ass.

Angie jumped on top of Ryan and brought her elbow down on his throat. His body jerked and convulsed as he struggled for air. Angie found herself wanting to savor the choking noises that came from him, but wasn't about to give him a chance to get the upper hand. With both hands, she grabbed him by the hair, pulled his head off the floor, then threw it back down. She did it again, then again.

His eyelids fluttered, then closed as his mouth tried to form words.

Then he went still.

Angie came to her senses and carefully checked his throat for a pulse. It was weak, but there. She suddenly felt weak again and climbed off of Ryan. The adrenaline rush had faded, and she had to fight the urge to lie down and sleep. She searched Ryan's unconscious body, looking for his cell phone. He didn't have it on him.

She got to her feet and staggered to the outside door, opened it, and walked out into the daylight.

Chapter 8

"His phone wasn't in the car, either. Weird for him, he never goes anywhere without it."

Angie looked down at her plate of Lo Mein, which she'd been unconsciously twirling with her fork. "He would have been in a big hurry, I guess."

Across the booth from her, Carol Drake took a sip of her Diet Coke and then folded her hands. "At least he left the keys in the ignition."

Angie forced a bitter smile. "Yeah, there's that."

They sat in silence a moment.

"Is there going to be a trial?"

Angie shook her head. "I don't know. His lawyer is trying to work out a deal. Second-degree murder instead of first-degree, along with everything else. Who knows if it'll fly? At the very least, they can't make a wife testify against her husband, so no matter what happens, I won't have to take the stand."

"Ah. So, that's why you haven't divorced him."

"Yep."

When they finished eating and the check came, Carol insisted on paying. Angie didn't battle her over it as she might have in better days. The four weeks of work she'd missed had hit her bank account where it lived, and it would be a long while of ramen noodle dinners and life without cable before she once again stood on solid ground.

They made their way to the parking lot, where their cars were parked side by side.

"Come over here a second," Angie said.

Carol followed her to the driver's side of her car.

"Got a present for you."

Carol smirked. "Oh? And what might that be?"

Angie opened the back door and pulled out the rolled-up quilt.

"I don't know if you intended this as a loan or a gift, but either way, you can have it back."

Carol looked at the quilt, then at Angie. She gave her an understanding look and took the quilt in her arms.

"Angie? I guess I should say I'm sorry ..."

Angie held a hand up. "Don't. All that thing did was show me what I should have seen three years ago."

A smile formed on Carol's face, then fell. She looked down.

"You know, sometimes when I think about my ex-husband, about how things ended up, sometimes I think it would be nice if I could just go back and erase all of it. All the things that made me suspicious of him in the first place, you know?"

Angie looked off to the side. "Yeah, I know."

Carol hesitated before speaking again. "If you had a chance to do that, do you think you would?"

Angie took a moment, and then the corner of her mouth curled slightly upward. "I think, for the sake of my own sanity, I ought to leave that alley unexplored."

Carol nodded, and then walked around the rear of Angie's car. She turned back. "See you Monday, Ange."

Angie just waved, opened her car door, and got in.

ABOUT THE AUTHORS

Hal Bodner is a Bram Stoker Award-nominated author, best known for his best-selling gay vampire novel, *Bite Club*, and the lupine sequel, *The Trouble With Hairy*. He tells people he was born in East Philadelphia because so few people know where Cherry Hill, New Jersey is located. The first person he saw ever saw was the doctor who delivered him, C. Everett Koop, the future US Surgeon General. Thus, from birth Hal was ironically destined to become a heavy smoker -- a habit he greatly misses.

He moved to West Hollywood in the 1980s and has rarely left the city limits during the past several decades. In fact, he is so WeHo-centric that he cannot find his way around Beverly Hills, which is the next town over. In a burst of over optimism, he bought a six bedroom mansion in Highland Park, a supposedly up-and-coming area of East Los Angeles. After three years of watching the street gangs doing drug deals in his back yard, he fled back to WeHo.

During his sojourn in East L.A., he was protected from the harm because of his habit of chasing his escaped pet peacock down Figueroa Boulevard at night, dressed in his fluffy bathrobe and fuzzy Cthulu slippers while yelling "Apollo! Apollo! Come back!" None of the gang members would shoot him; they were laughing too hard.

His various professions have included stints as an entertainment lawyer, a scheduler for a 976 sex telephone line, a theater reviewer and the personal assistant to a television star. For several years, he owned Heavy Petting, a pet boutique where movie stars bought gold-plated water dishes and designer wardrobes for their Chihuahuas and Pomeranians.

In the erotic paranormal romance genre—which he refers to as "supernatural smut"—he is best known for having written *In Flesh and Stone* and *For Love of the Dead*. His comic gay super hero trilogy will hopefully debut shortly with *Fabulous in Tights*, to be followed by *A Study in Spandex*. He has recently agreed to write a series of mystery novellas featuring a gay detective and his Watsonian sidekick, who is the madam of a bordello.

Hal married a man roughly half his age who had no idea that Liza Minnelli and Judy Garland were related. In consequence, he has discovered that the use of hair dye is rarely an adequate substitute for Viagra.

Sebastian Bendix is a Los Angeles-based writer and musician, as well as host of a popular midnight horror film series, Friday Night Frights at the Cinefamily. He attended school at Emerson College for writing and has had pieces published in both in print (Mean Magazine, Sanitarium Magazine) and online (CHUD.com and Encounters Magazine). He has written several screenplays in the fantasy/horror genre, one of which, The Black Cradle, is in development as an independent feature. The Patchwork Girl was his first foray into the world of prose fiction. His second novel, The Stronghold, is nearing completion and will be out to publishers in 2015.

Russell Coy lives in Northern Indiana with his wife and daughter. Feel free to connect with him on Facebook, Goodreads, and Twitter.

And be sure to check out VOLUME 1!

Includes Richard Black's *Nikolis Cole: The Low-Rise Saint*, Sebastian Bendix's *Rock, Paper, Scissors*, and Joshua Rex's *Coattails*!

NOTE: Grave Markers are available individually in digital format or as a 3-in-1 print compilation.

www.ingramcontent.com/pod-product-compliance
Lightning Source LLC
Chambersburg PA
CBHW051239170626
46809CB00004B/1395